The Alexis Stanton Chronicles
by
J.C. Phelps

Color Me Grey
Shades of Grey
Reflections of Grey
Traces of Grey
Fragments of Grey

J.C. PHELPS

FRAGMENTS OF GREY

THE ALEXIS STANTON CHRONICLES, BOOK 5

PUBLISHED BY
J.C. Phelps
Fragments of Grey
Copyright © 2014 by J.C. Phelps

Cover design and formatting by TERyvisions

ISBN-10: 0981769055
ISBN-13: 978-0-9817690-5-9

NewPub Binding, USA

Contents

Written for

Alexandra
Edy
Ellie
Jim
Rick
Robert
&
Robert

Special thanks to

Becky - Bobbe - Caroline - Dawn - Deb - Erin - Jen
Jessica - Jimmy - John - Julia - Karen - Kathy
Kelly - Linda - Lorna - Lynn - Mac - Natasha
Robert - Tamara - Terry - Val

A huge thank you to LK Rigel and all the work you did for me, including writing my dreaded description. Thank you to all of my early readers, alpha, beta, and editors. Without you I wouldn't have had to courage to press that publish button.

I'd like to express an extra hearty thank you to Caroline, Linda, Mac and Terry. THANK YOU!

For my Ranger friend—you know how much of a help you are to me, as well as a source of happiness for my entire family.

Fragments of Grey

Book Five of the Alexis Stanton Chronicles

By

J.C. Phelps

Chapter One

PUBLIC EXECUTION. THAT'S WHAT THE instructions had specified.

Vasile Mitu, some sort of midlevel Romanian criminal, had really pissed off someone by trafficking women and children. I wondered if it would have been overlooked if he hadn't snatched up a government official's niece.

I really didn't care. Colin had done all the research on this one and filled me in on the details. All I wanted was to be kept busy. And as far as I was concerned, all human traffickers deserved to be made an example of, so I was more than happy to oblige.

The problem that faced me at the moment had nothing to do with research or my wanting to fulfill the contract, it had to do with fulfilling the contract completely.

The target had picked up and moved to a remote mountain cabin shortly after I arrived in the country more than a month ago. The opportunities to remove him were often and ideal, but the *public execution* part of the contract stayed my hand. If there had been no stipulations, I would have been off this mountain the day I arrived. I hoped today would be the day.

The pungent smell of dirt near my face mingled with the trees. The scents and the vision of the small building tucked away on the side of the mountain had been triggering memories I'd been trying to repress. I missed roughing it in the mountains. I missed the cabin. I longed for things that would never be.

No matter what I missed, this was where I was. This was what I did. Thankfully, Colin seemed to find me a lot more jobs than White ever did.

White had been more selective than Colin, but my priorities had changed. Back then I had other things I needed to do and other things to keep my attention. Penumbra was a side business. Now it was all that I had. All that I was.

Of course, none of my recent work was done as Penumbra. Even if the jobs had been there, I told Colin I'd rather keep Penumbra quiet for a while. He didn't fully understand, but he didn't question me.

After that fateful meeting at White and Associates, telling my partners I was Penumbra in my spare time, I kept my head low and my location quiet. But I still kept in close contact with White for a few weeks, hoping I'd find an excuse to return. Any reason to forgive Red would have been enough, but he didn't budge in his conclusion that I'd somehow betrayed them all by hiding the fact I was Penumbra. I wasn't sure what he might do. I didn't believe he'd go public, but the notion played around the edge of my thoughts.

I brought my concerns up with White in a moment when I was ready to give in and go back. If he'd have asked me one more time, reassured me he'd bring Red around, I would have given in.

"Give him a little more time to work through this," he said instead.

"If he shows any signs of going public, I'll have to do something." I was angry White hadn't continued to beg me to come home, and the threat just popped out.

"It might be best if you stay away for a bit yet," was all he said.

The line was quiet as I digested the fact White had completely sided with Red.

My last words to White were, "Keep your dog leashed or you'll find yourself at the pet cemetery." I hung up and instantly regretted what I'd said, even if I meant every word. If Red threatened me or my family, I'd have no choice. Surprisingly, I was okay with this. Yet I knew the deep loyalty my partners had for each other. I knew my serious threat built a wall between me and them. My anger made me vocalize something we all knew, but something that shouldn't have been said if I wanted to continue being a part of White and Associates. White would have no other choice but to protect his partner. I imagined his loyalty to me falling to his feet like a pile of sand.

I realized then I could put all of my emotions aside in an instant. Even my deep love for White was muted. All of this opened a hole in my heart, but I knew, after I hung up on White, I'd live without them.

I buried myself in jobs, cut all ties with everyone except Colin, and walked away from my home. I kept up on my surveillance of White and Associates—and Red in particular—through Colin. I still hadn't told Colin what had transpired because I didn't want him or my father to take action. If it came to that, I'd do the job. I *wanted* to do the job.

Even if the emotion was quelled, small drips escaped to keep the well below rippling. The phone I'd bought specifically for communicating with White was shut off, but I still couldn't bring myself to toss it.

I knew it wasn't a good idea to have any identifying objects on me while doing a job, but I still carried it with me everywhere. It was in my back pocket right now.

Deep down I held hope of going home. I didn't want to toss my hope away, and I was afraid of losing my only link back to a world I loved. Part of my reasoning was I'd added all kinds of fun things to it. Thanks to my additions, I could utilize the GPS functions without a connection, and it could come in handy in a dark place.

I wanted to curl up into a ball and cry the days away. I wanted White to track me down and make everything okay. I wanted so much that just was not possible any more.

My threat to Red was the end. I knew my partners had an unbreakable bond, and nothing could intrude upon that loyalty, least of all an outsider.

The gradual dawning of the sun behind me pulled me from my depression. The rays had not yet touched the side of the cabin that morning, but as it became brighter my anxiousness became stronger.

Vasile had established his routine very early after moving to his cabin. He was up within half an hour of the sunrise and on his computer within half an hour of getting out of bed.

It took me a couple days to think about repositioning myself to see exactly what he was doing on the computer. He made regular video calls to the same person and after watching them for a couple weeks I knew he was to have a conference call with several of his *partners in crime* this morning. I'd use this as my public display.

I'd come closer in the night so I could gain access to his cabin shortly after I took the shot. My ghillie suit had to mimic this terrain perfectly. I'd gone all out and even disguised the soles of my shoes. He had a habit of gazing out his windows with a cup of coffee in the morning and I would be directly in his line of sight.

Anticipation boiled in my stomach as I watched the sun creep up on the cabin. Deep breaths and mentally walking through my plan worked to keep me sitting perfectly still.

Not long now.

Vasile was out of bed making his way to his computer. He switched it on like every other morning, and went to the kitchen to make his coffee. Within minutes he stood at his window enjoying the scenery. I couldn't stop myself from mentally telling him to enjoy it, it would be his last chance. I also couldn't stop myself from feeling triumph over removing a blight from the human race.

His face was content and serene as he scanned his surroundings. The steam from his coffee swirled from the cup making me wish I had my own. Vasile's eyes brushed across me. There was no hint he picked me out, but I held my breath long after he moved from the window.

Deviating from his normal routine, he went back to his bedroom and pulled a plastic-covered suit from his closet. He laid it on the bed and smoothed out the plastic before he went to the bathroom and shut the door.

I didn't have a clear view from my location so every time he used the bathroom with the door closed it made me nervous. I wanted to know what he was doing in there. The only solace I had at these times was the fact that the bathroom window was too small for him to climb out of.

After many tense minutes he finally stepped from the bathroom stark naked. This wasn't the first time I'd seen Vasile in his birthday suit, but it shocked me every time. He was a fit man in his early thirties and it seemed a bit of a shame to deprive the world of a body like that. It was the brain I'd aim for, anyway.

As was my habit, *one shot, one kill,* started to loop through my thoughts. My finger wasn't on the trigger yet, but it still threatened to twitch. I took several deep breaths as I continued to watch Vasile prepare for his meeting.

He was clean-shaven with his hair slicked back. It looked as if he'd slathered in some kind of oil or mousse. I could clearly see where the comb's teeth had put tiny parts through his hair.

He stood for a moment, admiring his appearance in the full-length mirror that hung on the door between his bedroom and bathroom. With the suit on he had an air of ruthlessness. I didn't know what his thoughts were, but mine were, *at least the undertaker won't have to work too hard before putting him in his casket.*

I watched him practice several facial expressions, all of which gave me chills. I found myself cringing at the thoughts those expressions brought to mind. He was certainly nice to look at and the show of aggression on his face actually made him somewhat desirable—until I remembered what he did for a living. Chances were, any woman who found herself in a relationship with this man would soon find herself swept away from her home and family, living the rest of her life out as some kind of slave.

After some minor cleanup he signed in and started his video chat with the other man whose face had become familiar to me.

Soon, Vasile had several chat windows opened and the meeting began. I took one last serious look at the man who wouldn't see tomorrow, took in a deep breath, released the safety on my rifle, exhaled, and pulled the trigger.

The recoil moved me back a few inches, a feeling of satisfaction radiated from the slight pain I felt in my shoulder. I'd forgotten the feel of a .50 caliber. It felt good. Then the bullet reached Vasile. I watched as his head disappeared and his body was thrown from his chair.

That had not been my intention. I'd been using whatever Colin had made accessible to me and they happened to be much smaller caliber rounds. I should have considered the mess I was going to make when using Penumbra's signature rifle.

The impact had come from the side so the computer screen was still visible, though a little messy. Watching the full realization reach the four men on the other side of the screen was magnificent. It was only a matter of seconds before they realized what had happened and only a few seconds after that the computer screen went dark. If my contractor got to the computer before anyone else, it was highly possible they'd all be tracked down in short order.

I hurried to gather up my meager supplies and hiked down to the cabin. I'd intended to go in and drop my Penumbra packet on the chest of the dead man, but I decided against it when I saw the huge mess I'd made inside.

I passed Vasile's vehicle as I walked down the driveway back toward the cover of the trees. It tempted me. I had a full day's hike back to civilization. I resisted and continued to walk lightly to avoid leaving traces behind.

The sun was setting when I finally reached a road that led to a small town. I'd been slowly dismantling my ghillie suit and the .50 caliber as I walked, stopping every so often to bury another piece of the beautiful weapon. At least it wasn't the one that had been given to me by the men. I'd probably never see it again, but it was nice to know it was more than likely still in one piece. When I buried the last of the .50 caliber a wave of relief and sadness passed over me.

I looked myself over one more time and decided to change into the set of clean clothes I'd packed in with me. I still looked like I'd taken a tumble down a hill. A few sticks, leaves, and grass still clung to my clothes. I was glad to peel off the old clothes and put on something different for the first time in more than a month.

I opted to bypass the small towns and continued my hike back to the closest city with an airport. It was easy to stay out of sight until I got closer to the larger populated city. When I reached the airport I went directly to the bathroom to clean up.

The mirror reflected a face I hadn't seen in months. Though it was my own, I didn't remember the dark circles under my eyes. Cold water from the tap washed away the dirt and dust, but not the tired and drawn look. I felt fatigue seep into my bones as I examined myself. A few extra splashes of cold water and I walked with purpose to the ticket counter. The next flight left in just under an hour. I hoped I could hold out that much longer now that I was sedentary.

Chapter Two

I GOT PLENTY OF REST BETWEEN actual flight time and lay-overs before I landed as close to home as I dared. It felt good to be back on familiar ground.

I had the taxi driver make a few stops for supplies, like a new, prepaid phone, clean clothes, and toiletries before I had him drop me at a nearby hotel.

The first thing I did after I checked in was stand under the hot water in the shower for a full hour. Going without a real shower for more than a month is even harder than not changing clothes for that amount of time.

Time to check in.

I dialed Colin.

"Hey," I said.

"You're back?"

"Just."

"Everything go okay?" Colin's tone was always anxious after I did a job, but seemed even more on edge this time.

"I was unable to drop the packet, but the job's done. What's next?"

I was looking forward to my next job. It was too hard to sit alone in a hotel room for days at a time.

"That's actually a good thing. There was a problem with the intel for that job. I need you to lay low for a while."

"What problem with the intel?"

Panic was creeping up on me.

"Nothing for you to worry about. It's my problem, especially since you didn't drop the packet. That was a lucky break."

"Then why can't you put me back out?"

"I'm sorry, Alex. I don't have anything right now. Besides, your dad said you need to slow down."

"What? I need to do something. I can't just sit around. I don't have anything to fall back on."

"It won't hurt you to take a break for a couple months. You deserve it."

"A couple of months! Absolutely not!" Tears began to form in my eyes.

"Where are you?" Colin's voice became calm and even.

"I'm— I'm not far." I almost told him.

"Can we meet for dinner?"

"I'm not that close."

"Can you be close enough by tomorrow night?"

"I'm not telling you where I'm at, Colin. Quit trying to figure it out."

"I could just put a trace on your calls, you know." He threw back.

"Do you want me to hang up?"

"No. Don't. We're just worried about you. You've done seven hits in five months and you're asking for more. You *have* to tell me what's going on."

"I have." I evaded a full explanation.

"Come on, Alex. You haven't told me shit. I've been more than supportive and I haven't asked any questions. Now it's your turn to give a little to get a little."

"If I tell you why I left White and Associates you'll give me a job?"

"Maybe."

"You won't even commit to another job if I tell you what you want to hear?"

"I can't promise. It's out of my hands. The Admiral—"

"Screw you and screw the Admiral. The only thing you need to know is that I no longer work with White and Associates."

"Alex." He sighed heavily. "You've been on a solid run for months. You don't come up for air. You even quit calling White five months ago. We're all worried about you."

"You're *all* worried about me? You've been talking to White?"

"Of course I have. We have a partnership. Besides, your dad pulled him in for questioning."

"What do you mean, questioning?"

"Your dad wanted to know what was going on. Why you walked away and pretty much disappeared. Alex, you have to let us know if you're in danger."

"Is Red okay?" I asked reflexively.

"He's fine. Why?"

"How about the rest of the guys? Are they okay?" I tried to cover up my blunder.

"They are all just fine."

"What did White tell you?" I prodded.

"He said you overreacted to an internal matter. Your dad tried, but he couldn't get any details from him. I'm begging you. Tell me. The way you've been acting isn't healthy and I can't be a part of it any more unless I know the whys behind it."

"Maybe I did overreact, but I said some things I can't take back, even if I wanted to. The relationships are too damaged to be repaired and I can't go back. So, there's no point in pretending I could."

"What do you want me to tell White when he calls me in about an hour? He calls me every day at the same time to ask about you."

"White has no right to ask about me. He threw me aside for—" I took a breath before I said more than I wanted to. "Do me a favor, Colin. The next time White asks about me, tell him it's none of his business."

"Were the two of you a couple?" His words came out clenched. "Is he the real reason you left White and Associates?"

"No. Red is the reason I left and White is the reason I stay away. I didn't lie when I told you Red and I had a falling out. But, White standing behind Red and his bullshit is why I'm staying away. I couldn't work with them knowing I didn't have their full loyalty, like they expect from me. Is that good enough? Will you give me a job now?"

The line was quiet for a short period.

"Alex, I can't. I'm sorry."

"Colin, I need something to do. I can't just sit here in this hotel room watching T.V. I *need* something."

"Listen to yourself, Alex. You sound like an addict. Please, come home for a while."

"If I meet you for dinner to prove to you I'm fine can we talk about getting me back out there?"

"Of course."

"You have to promise it'll be just you and me."

"I promise. Just me and you. I promise. When?"

"I'll call you when I get there." I hung up.

I didn't look forward to going back to the city that held White and Associates, but I had to if I wanted to keep busy.

The phone I'd used to keep in touch with White was still in my back pocket. I pulled it out and turned it over in my hands. Colin said he called every day to check on me. I turned it on and stared at it. Finally, I put it on my side table, laid back on the bed and fell asleep.

I woke up before the sun, as usual, and took a shower before I called a car rental service. One of the hardest things I did right after I cut ties with White was sell my Mustang. Now I was traveling by rental car, taxi and bus. I'd worked so hard for that car and I loved it. But, the simplest solution had been to sell it. I got more for it than what I'd paid for it. The one thing that made it bearable was knowing that the men could track me to the new owner, but the trail ended there.

Last night I'd told Colin I wasn't close enough to meet him for dinner, but I was within an hour of the city. I never stayed more than two hundred miles from home while I waited for Colin to set up a new job.

I drove directly to Gabriella's house. I'd missed her and always had every intention of coming back to her. I'd only put it off because I couldn't bear to put myself anywhere near White. Since I was back in the city, I might as well pay her a visit.

I parked on the street and watched her putter around her house for half an hour before I mustered up the courage to knock on her door.

"Alex!" She pulled me into a tight embrace and then pulled me into the house. "Where have you been? What's going on? Do you want some coffee?"

"Coffee sounds wonderful." I plopped down on the couch and waited for her to bring it to me.

I sat forward to take the coffee from her and held it in both of my hands for the warmth. I felt strangely cold.

She took a seat on her coffee table directly in front of me and waited quietly for my answers. I took a light sip of the coffee before I spoke.

"How have you been?"

"I'm great. Martin asked me to marry him."

"You're getting married?"

"Eventually. But, that's not the current topic. We'll get to that later."

She waved it away and hit me with raised eyebrows.

"Well, after I quit White and Associates I took some time to readjust."

I shrugged.

"Whoa. Back up." She stood. "You quit?"

It was my turn to raise my eyebrows. "Yes. Didn't White tell you?"

"No. That son of a bitch! What the hell did he do?"

Her hands were on her hips now and her face was beet red.

I laughed at the sight. I knew she didn't have the training I did, but I didn't think I'd challenge her at the moment.

"It's okay, Gabriella. Take a breath." I stood up and rubbed her shoulder.

"I don't think I can work there any more." Tears stood in her eyes.

"Don't you worry about me, I'm better off. I'm making more money than I ever did and I'm my own boss."

"Who're you working for? I mean, can I come to work with you? I need a job because I just quit."

"I'm a private contractor now. I do things for my dad. And, I don't think you should quit your job. This has nothing to do with anything but me."

"White had to have done something. I know how much you love him and you wouldn't just walk away without a good reason." She was working herself up into a full-fledged tantrum. She started pacing in front of the couch.

"I mean, how could you quit? You'd just finally gotten together with him. Tell me. I want to know what the hell he did to you. Did he cheat? I wouldn't have ever guessed him as a cheater, but men can be sneaky assholes. He didn't hit you, did he? If he hit you I'll kill him. Seriously, I'll go to work and poison his fricking coffee."

"Gabby!"

I never called her Gabby but I needed less syllables to get her attention.

She stopped in her tracks, set her feet and demanded, "Well? What the hell happened?"

"I just got fed up with Red. I can't work with him, and White will always side with him. I can't work with people who don't respect me. And I most definitely can't *be* with a man who will choose someone else over me, even if I'm wrong. *But,* I wasn't wrong."

"Oh honey," she pulled me in for another tight hug. "Are you okay?" she mumbled into my hair.

"I'm fine, Gabriella."

She released her grip on me and stepped back.

"I'm sorry White didn't tell you I'd quit. I really thought he would have by now."

I wiped a tear from her face. She was taking this harder than I thought she would. "I'm going to be in town for a few days, maybe we can have dinner and catch up."

"Of course we'll have dinner. Where are your bags? You're staying with me," she said.

"Oh, no. I can't."

"It's no trouble. Get your bags and I'll get you all set up."

"No, Gabriella. I really can't. I haven't talked to White for five months and he's been trying to find me. I don't want the hassle and I don't want to pull you into any drama."

"Why would White know you're here?"

"I'm not saying you'd tell him, but you know how he just *knows* things."

"He won't get anything out of me. I'm never going back to that building until you do."

"You can't really quit your job."

"Watch me, sweetie. I've got plenty of money saved up. Plus, when I'm ready, I can find a job anywhere. I've got mad skills."

She mimicked her typing ability in the air.

"Don't quit your job, Gabriella." I shook my head. "It's all good. You don't need to make a statement on my behalf. Besides, if you quit today, it'll only draw attention and then we couldn't even meet for dinner later."

Her shoulders slumped. "Fine, but I'm not getting him any coffee for a month."

"Do me a favor?"

"Anything, hon."

"Don't get Red coffee ever again?"

"You know it! Did you want me to let Black know you're okay?"

My breath caught in my throat and my lip quivered before I could control it.

"Nah. I'd rather no one knows I'm here. I've got to get going." I walked to her phone table and wrote my latest pre-paid phone number on the pad next to the phone. "This is my current number. You can call me later and we'll decide where to meet for dinner."

We hugged one more time before I left. Her embrace was actually tender this time around and almost made me break down. I held it together long enough to get into my car and drive exactly two blocks before I had to pull over to control my shaking.

Black. I'd absolutely refused to allow my mind to wander to him. But his name instantly brought back the vision of his face when he found out I was Penumbra. His eyes were filled with disbelief and sadness. It made me sick to my stomach to remember it. It hurt him to find out I'd kept this from him. I knew, when I saw his reaction, he thought I would have told him and I wished I had. My secret would have been safe with him, probably safer with him than any other person on the planet.

My partners were closer to each other than brothers, and Black was the one man I shared that same type of relationship with. I should say I used to share that kind of relationship with him. Now—

I forced myself to get it together. There was nothing I could do about it now. Absolutely nothing.

Chapter Three

MY HEART POUNDED AS I registered at the hotel's front desk. At a glance, there was nothing different about this hotel. Even if the lobbies might vary somewhat all hotels were essentially the same. I'd become accustomed to living in them. It was like having the same apartment where someone came in and rearranged the furniture and changed the bedding, carpet and wallpaper every so often. The only thing that made this hotel any different from all the others was that it was only three blocks from White and Associates.

I holed up in my room for several hours before I decided to venture back out into the city. My nervousness was starting to aggravate me. I am Penumbra, for crying out loud. I used to be Ms. Grey. I should be afraid of nothing, especially not my ex-partners. Still, I knew I wasn't ready to see any of them face to face. Nothing violent would happen, but I wasn't ready to face the heartbreak, the loneliness of being on my own for the first time in my entire life.

Outside the lobby I hailed a taxi and had him drive me to the nearest salon. The stylist begged me to try a less drastic change when I told him I wanted all my hair cut off.

"No. This is something I've been meaning to do, anyway." I reassured him.

"You have to be absolutely certain before we do this."

"I am. Go for it. I'm looking forward to a new hair style." I lied. I didn't want to cut my hair. It was the one thing about me that had never changed. I'd always worn it long. I had no idea how to care for a short do. But, I was rebelling, in a way. I wasn't the same person who used to live in this city, why should I look like her?

The stylist pulled my hair back into a ponytail and stood staring at the bundled hair in his hands for a few seconds.

"You're sure?" He made eye contact through the mirror.

I nodded.

With a sad sigh he reached for his scissors and brought them to the back of my head.

"When we're done it'll only be about this long."

He leveled his hand near my chin.

"Sounds good." I forced a smile.

"Okay—"

Twenty minutes later I looked entirely different. I felt lighter. No more braids, no more buns. No more Alexis. I smiled.

Instead of hailing a cab I took a walk. My confidence was back, full force. I'd been worrying about Colin not giving me any more jobs. Truthfully, I didn't know what I'd do if he didn't. Still, at this exact moment, I didn't care. Maybe I was the opposite of Samson and my hair held my weaknesses and not my strength.

My smile broadened at the thought. I couldn't remember the last time I wore a true smile of happiness, rather than one of satisfaction from a job well done. I held my head higher and practically bounced down the sidewalk. My hair definitely bounced. It was freeing.

After only a couple blocks I gave in and hailed a cab. I wanted to do some shopping. I kept the driver occupied for a couple hours and tipped him well when he dropped me back at my hotel.

I hauled my packages into my room and set my prepaid cell on the dresser by the television. Gabriella should be calling me soon and I didn't want to hunt for the phone in the clutter I was sure to create when I started laying out my purchases.

I was looking forward to hearing her wedding plans and intended to take her to a nice restaurant to celebrate. The clothes I bought would probably be left here when I left the city, but I wanted some regular clothes instead of walking around looking like I still worked for a private military corporation.

Of course, I bought a couple sets of clothes that fit that description, but I'd take those with me.

The liberating feeling from cutting off my hair was starting to dissipate and I didn't want it to. Everything was still uncertain. The only thing I knew with certainty was that I'd meet with Gabriella this evening, take a few days to play with my laptop, then call Colin for our meeting.

My future was in his hands. I didn't like that.

He'd either have a new job for me or—what? Or what? The spending spree and makeover helped me realize, even if I was alone, I had enough money to be alone comfortably.

Though being alone for the first time in my life was somewhat freeing, it was still a daunting thought. I didn't want to wander the world all alone. I didn't want to take random classes for the rest of my life. I wanted to make a difference. I wanted to *be* Ms. Grey and Penumbra. I wanted my life back.

No matter how hard I yearned for her, I knew Ms. Grey wasn't coming back to me. Red would make sure of that.

The thought of Red made my blood boil. He'd stolen everything from me, everything. I was separated from everything I loved in this world because of him. I'd fought with myself almost every day since I left. I wanted to confront him. Kick his ass. But I knew that wouldn't do me any good. He'd still be convinced I was someone not to be trusted and he'd keep putting that thought in front of my partners. I'd considered reasoning with him, but if White couldn't, what made me think I could? I had one more option. I could tell my dad. I was sure he'd fix it. I was also sure it wouldn't be an outcome I'd be happy with. Red would, most likely, disappear. My partners would know it was my father protecting Penumbra. Some of them might go missing, as well.

There was no way I would be accepted, forgiven, or brought back to the day before Red told my secret. All I could do was try and keep control of this new life I'd created. And, if I couldn't, I'd have to start over. Somehow.

Even with these thoughts flitting around in my head, the new laptop beckoned to me. I flopped on the bed next to the computer and pushed the button on the front. A small click let me know I could lift the screen and get started.

I was only three blocks away. Maybe I could pick up White and Associates' signal from here. Hopefully they hadn't changed any passwords or I'd have to hack in. I knew I couldn't get into the protected network of C.I.C., but I might be able to find *my* computer.

Within seconds I had the computer searching for nearby networks. I watched the cursor spin as it searched. It came back almost immediately with several networks. All of them were locked except the hotel's service, and no sign of White and Associates' network.

Damn!

I had no real reason for wanting to snoop in on White and Associates. It was just a way for me to feel a little closer to my old life.

My prepaid cell chirped at me from the dresser. I shut the laptop with a sigh before answering it.

Gabriella already had a place in mind and gave me the address. I told her I'd meet her in an hour and started my primping for our night out.

As expected, my new hairstyle was the main focus for the first few minutes. Then the conversation centered on Gabriella. We spent an enjoyable evening talking about Martin's proposal, and her acceptance. Flowers, colors, her ideal wedding dress and other wedding ideas were the main topics.

"None of this is set in stone," she admitted. "We don't even have a date, but I'd love it if you'd be one of my bride's maids. I'd ask you to be the maid of honor, but I know you don't have time for that role."

I promised I'd try to be available when the time came.

"We'll probably just run off and get it done. Just the two of us. But, it's fun to think of all the different themes I could use." Her eyes took on a dreamy stare. "The cake. You know?"

"Yeah."

But I didn't know. I wasn't like some of those girls you see on television. The ones who'd been planning their weddings since they were in grade school. I'd never given it much thought. I'd given marriage plenty of thought, but not the ceremony. It had never been about the ceremony for me.

"Actually, I've never thought that much about my wedding," I admitted. "I think I'd prefer to elope."

"Of course *you* would. You'd make a gorgeous bride, though."

The conversation included other small tidbits about Martin's family. I learned Leland, Martin's younger brother who had once been my blind date, had finally told his family he preferred the company of men. He did it at a family dinner with his significant other present.

"How'd that go?" I asked.

"Just how I hoped it would. The family already knew, even if they wouldn't admit it until he actually said it." She took a sip of her wine. "I wasn't the only one at the table who wasn't surprised. Which was nice. The last thing I wanted to do was tell everyone I already knew."

It took every ounce of my self-control not to ask direct questions about White and the rest of my partners, but I managed. To my disappointment, Gabriella didn't offer any news, either.

After we finished our dinner and a couple glasses of wine, she suggested we continue the evening at a club. I turned her down, saying I was too tired. She accepted my refusal without any complaint and gave Martin a call to pick her up. I waited outside the restaurant with her until Martin showed up, then hailed a taxi back to my hotel.

EARLY THE NEXT MORNING THE coffee shop offered me a chair close enough to get back into White and Associates network, but after logging in, I shut it all down. I stared at the screen for only a few seconds before making that decision. White didn't keep much on the accessible network, so I wouldn't get much from snooping. Plus, I didn't have any files on my computer that I couldn't live without. It was best to make a clean split and not become a stalker. Just knowing I could get in was enough for me. Instead, I ate a muffin and sipped on a cup of coffee for an hour before returning to my hotel room.

Once back in my room I searched around for a shooting range close to the city that wasn't affiliated with White and Associates. Mesa Security Services ran one less than thirty miles outside of city limits. It was classified more as a *facility* than just a firing range, but unlike White and Associate's training facilities, they were open to the public. They offered several classes in all kinds of fields, and even had a lodge to house their clients. I rented a room for one night, called a car rental service, and was on the road as soon as the car was delivered to the hotel.

Chapter Four

THE *MESA SECURITY* SIGN ABOVE the doors to the lodge fit the scene. It was huge and literally flashy. Made from copper, it still held a glint from the late morning sun. I could only imagine how blinding it could be first thing in the morning.

I heard almost-continuous gunfire as I walked from the parking lot to the building. Two overly large doors opened up into the lobby and I was immediately greeted with a waiting area. A couple overstuffed leather chairs and matching couch sat around a large steerhide that was being used as a rug. The only access further into the lodge were doors on either side of the front counter and I noticed they required a keycard.

Even though it was somewhat contradictory, the lodge embraced a rustic as well as a modern feel. The lobby boasted a grand feeling that went nicely with the air of superiority on the desk clerk's face.

Behind the desk and clerk was a glass elevator that rose up only one floor. I could see into the rest of the building through the elevator glass and the open loft area. There were no rooms visible. The reservations page online had said I could choose a room in the lodge or one of the several cabins or barracks areas. I'd chosen the lodge.

"I have a reservation." I placed my driver's license on the counter.

The clerk picked up my license and brought it to his computer. He wore a sharp, black suit over a white shirt with a maroon bow tie and a name tag that read *Matt*. He was observant, but he didn't have that honed look I'd become accustomed to. His look was more haughty than anything.

"Please fill this out, Ms. Grey."

He pushed a clipboard toward me and I balked for a split second. I hadn't used the Grey name for a long time, but it seemed fitting when I'd placed my reservations. Hearing someone else say the name aloud was a jolt.

The paperwork on the clipboard was the standard check in slip asking for name, license plate number, make and model of my vehicle, but it also included a waver for use of the facilities and I had to promise to use the weapons I rented only for training purposes on the ranges that were assigned to me.

The clerk checked all the places marked with the yellow highlighted **X** before he handed me my keycard for my room.

"We put you in a corner suite, Ms. Grey." He pointed to the door on my right. "Use the keycard to go through that door. You'll find your room, room 105, at the end of the hall."

I took the card from him, followed his instructions, and entered the hallway. Another keycard protected door was a short distance inside the hallway and led into the interior of the lodge. I stopped long enough to take a brief glance through the small, rectangular window. I'd had a better view from the elevator glass.

The suite was larger than what I'd been living in for the past six months and it was a nice change. The first thing I noticed when I walked in the door was the sitting room. It had a television, couch and a small table. On the table was a fruit basket. I dropped my duffel bag on the floor and went directly to the basket. The apple on top was calling to me. The cellophane crinkled as I tore it open and a small card fluttered to the table. It read: *Thank you for choosing Mesa Security.*

The basket also held several brochures. I plopped into a chair, took a bite of the apple and started flipping through the brochures. They were basically instruction manuals on how to utilize the facility.

The brochures didn't cover anything more than what I'd already seen on the website except one of them was a map of the facility. The weapons and equipment rental shop was located inside the main body of the lodge.

I finished my apple and tossed the core into the trash can near the door before I ventured out.

Once outside my room I slid my keycard into my back pocket only to have to dig it out again to enter the central area.

I left the hallway and entered into a man's world. It was undeniable. Awards and trophies were scattered throughout the huge room. Some were cups, some showed a shooter taking aim, but the ones I marveled at were the animal trophies. There were several different types of deer, mountain goats, bear, moose, birds, exotic animals, and even fish. It vaguely reminded me of one of those oversized hunting and outdoor gear stores.

The trophies and awards weren't the only things scattered about the open part of the building. Men sat at tables, in easy chairs, and couches distributed through the great room. Most of them pretended not to notice me, but a few were openly staring. The looks suggested I was intruding into their secret club.

With my chin lifted I strolled toward the weapons rental. I tried, but I couldn't contain the smug grin. I'd become accustomed to being one of the only women in the room who could hold her own with these men as well as accustomed to knowing that fact before the men did.

The man at the counter was helping another customer so I held back and looked at the tactical vests. There were only a couple available in my size that weren't pink camouflage.

"The self-defense classes start in half an hour in building three. I can have someone give you a ride if you need it." The man behind the counter addressed me after he finished with his customer.

"I'm not here for the self-defense class. Do you have any ranges open to walk-ons?"

"Range one is currently open to walk-ons. But that's a long distance range."

"That sounds good. What have you got for rifles?"

He cocked his head to the side. "Do you require an instructor?"

"Nope."

He started to explain each rifle behind him in simplified terms.

"How far is the farthest target on the open range?" I interrupted his explanation.

"A thousand yards."

"How about that AR-50 over there?"

He grinned openly. "That might be a bit much for your slight frame. How about—"

"No. I'd like to rent the AR and buy a couple boxes of rounds."

"I'm sorry. The AR can only leave the shop with an instructor. If you give me a moment, I'll see if anyone is available to accompany you to the range."

He looked as if he were on the verge of kicking me out of the building but he walked to a phone and picked it up. His voice was too quiet for me to hear what he was saying but I was still able to see his lips move.

"Yeah. I've got some girl here who wants to shoot the AR-50... I know... Okay, thanks." He hung up and walked back toward me.

"Jake'll be here in a couple minutes and I'll release the weapon and ammo to him, but I need your card to bill your room."

I reached in my back pocket again and retrieved the card. He swiped it and punched in a couple numbers on the keypad, then handed the card back to me. While he pulled the rifle off the wall I wandered around the area looking at the various items for sale.

Less than a minute later a man walked up to the counter. He wore a gray button-up shirt with the sleeves bunched up past his elbows and he had it unbuttoned a couple of buttons at the top, showing the collar of the white t-shirt he wore underneath. It went well with his jeans and boots.

The man behind the counter handed over the AR-50, two boxes of ammo, and nodded in my direction with some disgust.

"Ready?" The man who must have been Jake asked me. He also wore a look of disgust and exasperation.

When I nodded he said, "Follow me."

He carried the AR-50 and the ammo as if it weighed nothing. I guessed it probably weighed at least thirty-five pounds. I knew I could carry it, but was glad he'd done it. I'm sure the size of it in my hands would have been somewhat laughable to all the men whose heads were turned once again as we strolled past them.

Jake led me directly to a Jeep with the top down. He put the rifle in the back seat and slid behind the wheel as I got into the passenger seat. Nothing was said until we parked in front of the range.

"So, you ever fired an AR-50?"

He hiked his head back, indicating the rifle that wouldn't fit into the back seat if the top was up.

"Nope."

He shook his head. "Why didn't you ask for an instructor then?"

"Don't need one."

I was enjoying this.

"If you've never fired one you most certainly do need one. I can't let you fire this without some assurance you know what you're doing."

I stepped out of the Jeep and reached for the rifle.

"No you don't." He hurried out of the vehicle and placed his hand on the weapon before I could lift it out.

"What's the worst that could happen?" I asked him.

Again he shook his head. "Let's go. I'll walk you through it."

I smiled at him and followed. He carried the rifle to a partially enclosed area with counters and benches.

"Sit here."

"I prefer the prone position."

"Fine."

Jake carried the rifle to a mat that was set up a few feet from the enclosed area.

"Take the position."

He held the rifle out for me. When I took it from him he tossed the ammo to the ground near the mat.

I set the rifle up and pretended I didn't have a hostile man hovering over me as I flattened out on my stomach. It took me only a few seconds to load a round and find the target. I exhaled and pulled the trigger.

The bullet found its mark but I was a bit off. I readjusted and loaded another round.

"Whoa. Wait," Jake said.

He walked back to the enclosed area and got a pair of binoculars.

When he returned he gave me the go ahead and I immediately fired the next round. *Still a bit off.* I chambered another round and received no objections from my *instructor*.

I fired all ten bullets in the first box before Jake asked if he could give it a shot.

"Did you bring your own ammo? I'm not paying for you to play."

He raised his eyebrows and smiled. "Continue, then."

The remaining rounds were fired long before I was ready to call it a day, but my arm ached.

"Nice shooting."

His attitude had turned around and he smiled at me now. It was an infectious grin and more than a little flirtatious.

"Thanks." I handed him the rifle and finished policing my brass. "Are there any other ranges open?"

"First," he held out his hand. "My name is Jake."

"Alex. Nice to meet you, Jake."

"What are you in the mood for?"

"I could go for some pistol practice. It's been a while since I fired a pistol."

Jake drove us back to the lodge and told me to wait in the Jeep, he'd take the AR-50 back and get us a couple pistols and some ammo.

Ten minutes later he re-entered the vehicle.

"Alex Grey from White and Associates?" he asked accusingly as he turned toward me.

"Formerly from White and Associates, yes."

"That explains a lot. I thought you'd be older and... more filled out."

"What do you mean? More filled out?" I kept my temper in check. We were in a vehicle and I had no maneuvering room.

"More—" He struggled to find the right word. "Buff? Muscular? Butch? Maybe less feminine is more what I mean."

A slight eyebrow hike with a direct look gave me chills. I hadn't paid much attention to his appearance until he made this comment. Now I realized he would be a catch for *any* woman. Not to mention the deep resonating tones his voice carried. But no matter what he looked like or what he thought I looked like, I was anything but *just* a girl or even *just* a woman. I was Ms. Grey. He'd learn to look at me with *that* title instead of girl.

"I don't think you'd cause much of a challenge if I had room to move." I sneered at him.

"Hostile *and* cocky." He lowered his chin and looked up at me with green eyes and an ornery grin. He still thought he could win this fight.

"Hostile when cornered, and confident, not cocky. There's a huge difference." I'd moved so I was facing him and both my arms and hands would be useful.

"So, what brings a member of White and Associates to Mesa Security?" His shoulders were tensed and his smile was gone.

"I no longer work with White and Associates." I leveled my look to counteract his.

"Is that so?"

"Yep."

"Why? You had a sweet position there." His attitude lightened some.

"Maybe so."

"Ah—" He obviously thought he'd figured it out and I assumed he thought it was a falling out with a boyfriend. I didn't care what he thought, except that I no longer worked for White and Associates.

"So, should I get out or are we going to go do some target practice?"

I didn't appreciate the instant distrust my name brought on, but Mesa Security Services could possibly be a good contact for me at some point.

He looked at me as if he were trying to see my innermost thoughts. I returned the serious look until he turned the engine over.

We ended up utilizing a couple more ranges and I hedged most of his questions until we returned to the lodge.

"So, you're here for only one night?"

"Yep."

"Will you be back?"

"Am I welcome back?"

"Why wouldn't you be welcome?"

"I've been getting the third degree since you realized I used to work for White and Associates. If I had known there was such animosity between Mesa Security and White and Associates I would have chosen a different facility. I'd never even heard of you guys until this morning."

"It's more of a friendly competition," he corrected me.

I rolled my eyes. "Whatever."

"We'll take your money the same as any other person who walks in off the street." He shrugged.

"I might come back."

"I'd like that." His friendly smile had been lacking since he realized who I was, but now he seemed as if he were starting to open up again.

After my day of grilling questions I wasn't sure I would come back. However, I didn't know of any other nearby firing ranges that weren't in league with White and Associates.

I almost checked out and headed back to the city, but decided to stick it out. The television kept me occupied for most of the night. Jake's suspicion had me on edge and I couldn't sleep. Once the television was showing nothing but infomercials I switched to my laptop and started researching Mesa Security.

I hadn't logged into the government database with my Penumbra access for months, but I was curious. Even if I was no longer a member of White and Associates I knew they were the good guys. I didn't want to be stepping into something I couldn't step out of.

Mesa Security Services had been on the scene a year longer than White and Associates and were in direct competition with them. Of course, White and Associates almost always won the good contracts because of their connections. Mesa Security did have a few government contracts to protect heads of state who entered hostile territory, but they never won a large contract if it went through my dad.

White and Associates offered up training for some groups outside of their own troops, but that was what Mesa Security mainly did. They trained troops, they trained police S.W.A.T. teams. That, and take on precarious civilian contracts. So, even though they were a rival P.M.C. they worked the field differently and it seemed evenly broken up.

Mark Posner owned and operated Mesa Security Services. He was an ex-Navy SEAL instructor and was discharged with honors. Jake's last name was Jensen and he served at the same time my partners did, but he was discharged, with honors, before any of them. He went directly to Mesa Security Services and held a high position on the training side of the company. Definitely worth swallowing my pride long enough to form a friendship.

The sun started to peek over the trees. I'd done my time. Now it was time to get back to the city and get some sleep before I called Colin.

At the counter I found someone other than Matt with a much more relaxed attitude.

"Ms. Grey. You're up early. How can I help you?" His nametag read: *Chris.*

"Time to check out, Chris." I placed my keycard on the counter.

"As you wish. One moment please. I'll get your paperwork ready." He spent a minute or two on the computer and walked back toward the printer to retrieve the paperwork. But he picked up the phone before returning to the counter. Unfortunately he spoke into the phone with his back to me. "Forgive me, Ms. Grey. There seems to be an issue with your bill. I've called my supervisor and he'll be right down to clear this up for us."

"An issue?"

"Yes. Please, my supervisor will be down soon. Could you take a seat?" He motioned to the waiting area.

"I'm paying cash. There should be no issue." I insisted.

"He'll be here shortly."

He wouldn't budge.

Great. All I wanted to do was shoot some guns and get out of the city for a while.

Jake came through the doors a few minutes later.

"You're up early. Leaving us so soon?" He joined me on the couch.

"Yes, I have business in the city. What's wrong with my bill? I'm paying cash so there should be no issues."

"Nothing bad. We've decided to comp all expenses if you'll give me a phone number where I can reach you. If you're truly no longer working with White and Associates we could find a use for your skills."

"Is this a job offer?"

"Possibly."

I sat there for a few seconds, not knowing what to say.

"So, you going to give me your number?" He smiled at me.

"You think you're charming, don't you?" I couldn't help but smile back at him.

"I try." He wagged his eyebrows.

"For a possible job, right?" I brought the tone back to the serious side.

"Possibly."

"How about you give me your number. I'll call you if I have some free time."

"Works for me."

He walked back to the counter and brought back a business card.

"I wrote my personal number on the back of this card. But if you lose this card you can usually get to me through the number here. If I'm not here, they'll know how to get in contact with me. We'll set up your interview."

"Interview?"

"Well, of sorts. It'll be more of a test. We'll want to know where your strengths and weaknesses are so we can stick you on the right jobs."

"I see." I narrowed my eyes. "I'll keep you in mind."

"Please do."

I felt his eyes on me as I left the building.

Chapter Five

Jake Jensen was on my mind the entire trip back to the city and invaded my dreams as I slept the day away.

As soon as I rolled out of bed I dialed Colin's number.

"Alex?"

"I'm in the city. How about we meet in an hour."

"Sounds good." He chose the restaurant and said he'd make the reservation.

I used the hour to shower and try to fix my new hairdo. I still didn't know how to make myself look presentable and regretted not going with a pixie cut.

I made it to the restaurant before Colin did and was led to our table. I ordered a glass of wine and some shrimp hors d'oeuvres. I hadn't eaten anything since I had that apple at Mesa Security.

My appetizer showed before Colin and I didn't wait for him before I started eating. But he showed up before I could finish off the plate.

The look of shock on his face was unmistakable.

"You cut your hair."

"Good to see you, too." I touched my hair. "Yes. I needed a change."

"It looks good on you, but I'm going to miss your braids." He made a pulling motion.

He took his seat across from me.

"Alex, you're going to be pretty pissed off with me."

"Why?"

Colin didn't have to explain because I saw my father strolling across the room to our table.

"You promised it would be just you and me," I hissed at him.

"You know your dad. He insisted I include him. If I wouldn't have given in he would have just followed me."

I took in a deep breath and redistributed my anger. It wasn't that I didn't want to see my dad, I just didn't want to explain myself to him.

"Dad. How's Mom?" I greeted him when he reached the table.

"Good. How have you been?"

"Good. Care for any shrimp?" I offered up my appetizer to the two men in front of me.

They both took me up on my offer. Our waiter showed up, took their drink orders and our dinner orders. We made small talk until the meal showed up.

"I suppose we can get down to business now," my dad said as he cut a strip from his steak.

"We're prepared to offer you a job as an outside set of eyes for White and Associates. They just landed a transport job for one of our ambassadors. They'll need a sharp pair of eyes to scout ahead. You'll leap-frog with a few other men to make sure the road is clear for their convoy."

"No thanks." I shook my head.

"Why not?" Colin asked.

"You're trying to get me back in with White and Associates and I don't want to be there. It's not going to happen."

"Then you need to tell us why," my dad said.

"Nope. That's not going to happen, either. If you two can't take my word for it that it was really no big deal and I said a few things I won't take back, then I guess—" I let it hang.

"Your choice," the Admiral said.

The three of us ate in silence for several minutes before I asked, "So? This is it?"

"Looks that way," the Admiral said over a mouthful of food.

Colin wore a sick look but kept shoveling in his own dinner.

"What about—" I didn't want to say *Penumbra* aloud.

"What about her? You've ditched your handler and Colin doesn't have time to police you or do your research. He screwed up your last job. Did you know that Vasile was high on the list of the Romanian government? Higher than those that paid your contract? I really hope you covered your tracks very well. The government won't be covering that one up, they'll be searching for you."

"What?" I glared at Colin.

"Don't be mad at him, Alex. It was your fault. If you hadn't allowed him to do all your research this probably wouldn't have happened. Hell, White would *never* have even offered you that job."

My stomach churned. "Do they have any leads?"

"No. It seems you've done a good job of covering your tracks. This time. But, if you're going to be this negligent, I can't justify putting you out on any more jobs. I set this up the way I did for a good reason, Alex. Colin has too much on his plate to be your handler, simple as that. White *wants* to be your handler but because you kissed and he told, you've cut ties."

"That's not what happened." I remembered my father's tactics too late.

"So, what was the real reason for cutting ties?"

"Red pissed me off. White stood up for him, which pissed me off. I said some things I can't take back that pissed White off, and I refuse to work with Red." I put my guard back up and repeated what I'd already told Colin.

"That makes sense as to why you'd cut ties with White and Associates as a whole, but not White. He didn't take Red's side about Penumbra, did he?"

"No." I should have rehearsed this dinner. I was so sure it would be just me and Colin. Had I known my dad was going to show and interrogate me, I would never have come. My track record of trying to deceive my father was zero, and how many times I'd tried to get away with something—in his favor.

"Uh-huh. Alex. Does Red know about Penumbra?"

"No. I told you, I'm not going into any detail about this. It's a personal matter and nothing you two need to concern yourselves with."

"Were you and *Red* an item?" Colin's look of incredulousness almost made me laugh, but I played it straight. To let them think this was better than giving them a reason to believe Red knew something he shouldn't. I took a second to internally thank Colin for coming up with this for me.

"No." I should have taken acting lessons. I wanted to sound unconvincing without them knowing I was *trying* to redirect their thoughts.

"Alex and Red have never been an item, Colin." My father's eyes narrowed. "I have my answers. You can charge this as a business dinner." He threw his napkin over his unfinished food, stood, and came to my side. "Sweetie, I love you." He put his hands on my shoulders and bent down to speak quietly. "But we can't offer any more jobs to you until you return to White and Associates and Colin cannot be your handler any longer. You'll have to work through your problem with White and I would be more than happy to take care of your problem with Red."

"Red is not a problem."

"I'll be the judge of that. Call your mother." He left me sitting there scared to death. My father had always awed me, but he'd never frightened me until now. Colin was pale and a little perspiration stood out on his forehead.

"What are you going to do?" He pushed his plate away.

"Nothing, it seems." I also pushed my plate away. I wasn't able to even look at my food any more.

"Do me a favor, Colin?"

"I'll try."

"Don't let my dad do anything to Red? He really doesn't know anything." I lied, probably my most convincing lie ever.

"Then why won't you tell me what's going on? That is the only thing I can think of that would cause all of this."

"Use your imagination, Colin. I'm sure there are other reasons you can come up with. Any of them are fine by me. Just don't let my dad hurt my partners."

I left him sitting alone at the table.

BACK IN MY HOTEL ROOM, I sat on the edge of my bed turning White's prepaid cell in my hands. I had to call him. I had to let him know and the sooner, the better.

My mouth was dry as I waited for him to pick up.

"Where are you?" White's voice came to me for the first time in five months.

"I'm close. Listen. I just had a meeting with my dad and Colin."

"You told them?"

"No, but my dad knows. You're going to have to warn Red. The Admiral offered to take care of my problem with Red."

"What the hell were you thinking, Alex? Red has kept his mouth shut. He might still be pissed off because he was left out of the loop, but he'd never do anything to jeopardize you."

"Are you sure of that?"

"Absolutely."

We were quiet for a full thirty seconds.

"Are you coming back?" he finally asked.

"I can't. I want to, but I can't. No one trusts me and Red will do everything he can to stop the guys from ever trusting me again. But I would be willing to do more outside jobs if you'd be my handler again."

"I don't know, Alex."

"It could keep my dad off Red's back if we restarted this part of the relationship. We don't have to do much. I need to lay low for a while, anyway."

"I know you do. How could you have taken that job?"

"The guy was a human trafficker."

"No he wasn't, Alex."

"What?"

"You stopped doing your own research, didn't you." I could picture him shaking his head in disgust.

I had no response.

"I'm more worried about you than Red, now. Alex, please come back. We can protect you."

"What was his crime?" I asked, ignoring his plea for me to come home.

"He was the son of a controversial diplomat. That was his crime."

I hung up the phone and found myself hovering over the toilet for an hour while my phone rang every few minutes. When I'd purged my stomach of everything I'd ever eaten, I went back to the phone and turned it to vibrate.

I'd killed an innocent man and all because I couldn't be bothered with doing the research myself any more. I'd trusted Colin more than I'd ever trusted White, and I shouldn't have. I knew Colin was trustworthy, but being my handler had never been his job before. As the Admiral said, he wasn't meant to be my handler.

I went back to the bathroom and spent the night over the toilet.

Chapter Six

SEVERAL HOURS OVER THE TOILET did nothing for my mood. I dragged myself to the bed and decided to look up the man I'd killed. How many lives had I ruined by not doing my due diligence? I was supposed to save lives, but I hadn't saved any lives, just ruined them.

The laptop waited expectantly, but I couldn't bear to open it. Instead, I curled up on the bed with the computer and White's phone next to me. The phone vibrated every half an hour or so, reminding me I could never make up for this. I wanted it all to stop, just stop being me.

I don't know how long I stayed on the bed in that position. I remembered telling housekeeping to leave me alone more than once. I finally gave in and made my way back to the bathroom.

I glanced in the mirror. I didn't recognize the person staring back at me. She looked pathetic and sickly. Dark circles under her eyes, pale, and thin. Not the way a trained killer should look. Maybe the way a serial killer would look. I sneered at myself in the mirror and stripped down. The shower helped wash away some of the pain, but I still couldn't cry.

When I exited the shower, I noticed White's phone had vibrated off the sink counter and onto the floor. The back of the phone had come off and the battery was underneath the toilet. I put it back together after I dried off and dressed. It vibrated in my hands immediately. I didn't answer it. Instead I shoved it into the back pocket of the jeans I'd found on the floor when looking for some clothes to wear.

Something stopped the phone from sliding in easily as it had always done before. I pulled out Jake's business card and turned it over. After a full minute of contemplation, I dialed his number.

He answered on the first ring. "Hello?"

"Jake?"

"Yes?"

"This is Alex Grey. I was wondering if your offer was still good."

"Of course it is. When do you want to meet?"

"Now?"

"Okay. I'm at the gym on the corner of 1st and Grand. Can you meet me there?"

"That's Helix's gym."

"You know Helix?"

"A little." I double-checked the time. Black should have been there and gone several hours ago. "Okay. I can be there in a few minutes."

I packed up what I wanted to keep and checked out of the hotel. I had no intentions of staying in the city after my meeting with Jake, regardless of what he may or may not offer me.

I took a taxi to the gym and carried my duffle bag in with me.

"Hey, beautiful." Helix's booming voice greeted me from across the building. "Where the hell have you been? Black's been in every morning without you for months. Plus, he gets downright pissed when I ask him where you're at." He lifted me for a tight hug. I could see Jake coming our way over Helix's shoulder.

"I left White and Associates." I managed to squeak out.

Helix stopped hugging me and stepped back quickly. "You're shittin' me, girl."

"Nope. It was time for me to get out on my own."

"No wonder Black's been foul lately." He turned to see Jake joining us. "Hey. My man, Jake. I'd like you to meet Ms. Grey."

"We've met." His smug smile irritated me for some reason. "Ready to show me what you've got?"

"You ain't going to work for Jake, are you?" Helix asked me.

"I don't know yet. Why? Do you recommend I steer clear?"

Helix looked at Jake and then back to me. "It's just a switch from White and Associates. A different take on the same job." He grinned at Jake who winked in return.

"Shall we?" Jake invited me to a mat with a wave of his hand.

"Boy. She's going to kick your ass," Helix said.

"Doubt that, big boy," Jake threw to Helix.

Now I had something to prove and plenty of anger to vent.

Jake lunged for me before I had my bearings, and I fell back on my butt as I tried to dodge. He gave me that same smug grin that irritated me earlier. I jumped back up and resumed my relaxed stance. This time he didn't come right for me and we stalked each other around the mat a few times. Eventually, he gave in and came at me again. I was ready and met him head on with a sharp jab to his gut. I managed to double him over, but he recovered almost immediately and grabbed me by the waist as I tried to sidestep.

He pulled me in for a bear hug from behind. My hands were free, so I used his forearms around my stomach to lift myself as high as I could. I threw my head back and made contact with his face. I heard the crunch of his nose as I wrapped my legs backwards around his knees. His grip didn't loosen, but he fell forward. I was able to break our fall somewhat with my outstretched hands and my knees. Jake's weight crushed me to the mat. I felt his face hit the back of my head again. The force caused me to do a face-plant into the mat.

Jake was still as his body pinned me to the mat. My head hurt like hell and I couldn't see through the tears. I tasted blood and knew my nose was broken.

"Holy shit!" Helix was at my side in an instant and lifted Jake off me. "I've never seen you play dirty before. You're good at it. Someone bring over the smelling salts," he ordered.

Within seconds, Jake was reviving. I kneeled next to him, dripping blood from my nose.

"Hey!" Helix yelled again. "Someone get my girl a towel and an ice pack."

"What the fuck was that?" Jake sat up, all smugness gone.

"That was me winning the fight," I said.

"She sure as hell did. I told you, Jake. She was going to kick your ass. You should always make nice before you spar."

Jake jumped up and resumed his fighting stance. I stood and wiped the blood from my face with my arm. He did the same with his own arm, creating a smear of blood from his nose to his ear.

It was my turn to give a smug smile. I was more than ready to kick someone's ass, or get mine kicked. I really didn't care at the moment. All I wanted to do was hit something, hurt something.

"Hey, you two. I think you both need a short break." Helix tried to intervene.

"Sorry, Helix. I'll try not to bleed too much on your mat." I said.

"That's not up to you." Jake glared at me. He was mad and I loved it.

"Oh, but it is, Jake."

We sparred for another fifteen minutes before either of us made significant contact again. He got me with a jarring slug to my gut. I doubled over, my breath gone. But, instead of stopping to hold my stomach like most people do, I rolled with it and came up behind him. I was still out of breath, but I managed to climb up his back in just two steps. I sat on his shoulders and then flipped myself around so when I looked down I could see his face between my legs.

He was actually smiling, though he had to know what was coming next. I threw my weight back and dropped him face first onto the mat. He came up bleeding all over again.

He wiped his nose again and held up his hand. "I'm impressed and more than a little turned on."

"I'm not done." I continued my advance.

Someone touched me lightly on my shoulder. "It's just me, girl," Helix said. "Don't hit me, but you should maybe give him a break. Ambulances in the parking lot are never good for business."

"Helix is right. How can I give you a job if you put me in the hospital?"

I came back to my senses and realized the gym was quiet. This wasn't the first time I'd stopped time in Helix's gym, but this was the first time I actually sparred with someone with every intention of hurting my partner rather than just getting the best of them, and the first time the crunch of breaking bones was a welcomed sound instead of something that made me cringe.

"Sorry, Jake. Cease fire?"

"Yes, please." He grinned.

"Next time you'll take my word for it, won't ya, Jake," Helix said.

"That I will, big boy." Jake and Helix clasped arms, both laughing. I was still angry, but I graciously accepted the wet towel that was offered by some hesitant hand. The blood I wiped from my face covered the towel. The gym doctor had made his way over to check Jake. He was shining a light into his eyes when he asked me if I ever lost consciousness.

"Nope," I replied through the towel I now held to my nose.

"Pinch your nose," the doctor said.

I nodded. "He going to be okay?"

"I think so." The doctor grinned at me.

"Black's going to be so proud," Helix boomed.

"Helix. Please. Don't tell Black I was here."

"If I don't, someone else will and then I'll have *him* on my ass. Sorry, Chicky. No can do."

"I guess I can't hold it against you."

The doctor came over to me with his light and started shining it in my eyes.

"You're good, too." He patted me on the back before he walked away.

"So. She got the job, Jake?"

"Only if she wants it," Jake responded in a nasally voice. Both of us were still pinching our noses to stop the blood flow.

"Depends on the job," I answered.

"Thanks for your hospitality, Helix, and sorry for the mess." Jake indicated the bloodied mat.

"Yeah. Sorry, Helix."

"Too bad we never hit it off. Now that you're running with a different crowd, maybe you'll change your mind. We still have to have our second date."

I laughed. "I'll call you, Helix." I handed him my bloodied towel and Jake did the same.

"Let's talk." Jake touched my arm and hiked his head toward the door.

I followed Jake out the door and into his new Dodge Charger.

"Nice car. Do you have any tissues? My nose is bleeding again." I held my head up in an attempt to divert the flow away from his upholstery.

"Mine too. I should have something in the glove compartment." He pointed.

I opened the compartment and pulled his 9mm onto my lap so I could dig out the fast food napkins he'd shoved in there.

"Here you go." I handed him a few napkins and kept a couple for myself before I replaced the weapon and shut the compartment door.

He smiled and shook his head as we held the paper towels to our noses.

"What?" I didn't understand the joke.

"I'd heard a lot about you and your attitude, but I thought it was all talk. Now I know better. You're a pistol."

"Not always." I didn't know if he could see my smile under the napkin or not.

"I could use a drink or an aspirin." He started his car and drove us away from the gym. "So, you and Helix dated?" he asked as we made our way through traffic.

"Not really. He had White line up a date for us as payment for something he did for White and Associates."

"Really? I bet that didn't go over well."

"I had a good time with Helix, but you're right. It didn't end well for White."

Jake asked me to fill him in on what training I had and what I thought my strengths and weaknesses were. I gave him a brief resume and told him that hand-to-hand fighting was probably my weakness.

"You'll never get the best of me again," he said.

"We'll see."

He'd driven us to a small bar not far from White and Associates' office building.

I followed behind him once again as we entered the bar.

"Yo, Jake."

The bartender greeted him as we stepped in.

"You okay?" he asked after Jake and I sat at the end of the bar. "Did you have an accident?"

"Nah, Merle. We're good. Just don't piss her off."

I looked at Jake. His eyes were starting to blacken. I wondered if mine were, too.

"You sure you don't need me to call Posner for you?" Merle asked.

"Yep. Just give me something strong. What are you drinking?" Jake asked me.

"Jack on the rocks, to start, please."

Merle grinned at my request. "Need some painkiller?"

"Yeah. Thanks."

Merle set our drinks in front of us and left us alone to chat.

"So, what's the real story? Why'd you quit White and Associates and why did they let you go?"

"First of all, they had no choice, and I quit for personal reasons."

"I want to know those personal reasons."

"Well, you're not going to hear them."

"You have a fling with Black that didn't work out?"

"No. Black was my mentor."

"He's a big son of a bitch. He comes in here from time to time."

"Great."

"You left on bad terms?"

"Kind of. White has asked me to come back, but the rest of the men haven't said anything."

"So, what made you pursue this line of work?"

"I don't know. I'm a good shot?"

"That you are."

The conversation switched over to what kinds of jobs I might find myself doing.

"We'll start you out slow," Jake said.

"When's my first job?"

"That's up to Posner and your past affiliation with White and Associates is a bigger bother for him than it is for me. He wants me to offer you an instructor's job to begin with. It'd help if you moved into a company facility so he could keep an eye on you."

"Keep an eye on me? Nah. That ain't happening."

"You gotta give a little to get a little," he said.

I downed my Jack. "I'm sick of hearing that." I knew I'd have done better recently if I'd had a babysitter, but I didn't want Jake or this *Posner* to take on that role. I waved at Merle to refill my glass even though I was already feeling the effects of the first one I'd been nursing.

"It'll be easier for you to stay at the facility while you're an instructor. I stay there." Jake grinned.

"Is that supposed to entice me?" I laughed.

Jake just shrugged, grinned, and took a sip of his whiskey.

I downed my second Jack in two gulps. The ice had melted and the booze was a little watered down. "Sorry, Jake. Not working for me."

"You plan on taking Helix up on that second date?"

Again I laughed. "That doesn't work for me either."

I waved Merle over again. "One more, Merle?"

Merle refilled the booze, but not my ice so the Jack was just that, Jack. He stood in front of us with the bottle in hand, waiting to refill Jake's glass. Jake downed his own drink and motioned for another. In two gulps I finished off the drink. It took my breath away.

"Coffee?" I half squeaked and half whispered as I held my hand over my empty glass.

"Not a big drinker?" Jake threw back his own drink and asked for another after my cup of coffee arrived.

"I'm a little drinker," I joked.

Chapter Seven

I WOKE UP IN A PANIC. As far as I could tell, the place was unfamiliar to me, but I couldn't open my eyes all the way.

I bolted up to a sitting position and was hit with a wave of nausea and a sharp headache. Moaning, I held my head with both hands for two seconds.

I felt movement on the bed next to me and was able to make out Jake. He'd rolled over to face me. I did a quick check to make sure I wasn't naked. Thankfully, I was fully clothed. Blood from my nose and Jake's still coated my shirt and pants.

"Man, I feel like crap," he complained as he sat up slowly.

"Where are we?"

"My room at Mesa."

"Your room?" I didn't know it was possible, but I felt even more sick.

Jake was decidedly a good-looking man, with all the attitude I liked in a man, but I didn't want to turn into a whore as well as a murderer. The night came back in blurry snippets. I remembered drinking two cups of coffee while we chatted and then going back to the booze. I also remembered talking with more people than just Jake.

"Don't worry. I'm certain, if something happened between us, I'd remember it, and so would you." He forced a smile. "I need food."

I hadn't eaten for days but the mention of food made me shiver in disgust.

"You look like hell, by the way." Jake's eyes were swollen almost shut.

"How can you tell? Can you even see?"

"I'm used to looking through swollen eyes. This isn't my first broken nose."

A pounding on Jake's door about sent me running to the bathroom.

Jake groaned again and rolled off the bed. "I'm coming."

He opened the door to a man who looked familiar, but I couldn't remember his name.

"You two look terrible. I brought you some ice packs and breakfast." The man entered the suite with a food trolley.

"Thanks, Joe." Jake took an ice pack from him and flopped into a chair at his table.

"I know I told you this last night, but I love that you kicked his ass," Joe said to me while putting the plates out on the table.

"I'm sorry, Joe. I don't remember much from last night."

"You were both already ten sheets to the wind by the time the fight broke out. Next time you pick a fight with Black, I'm staying home."

"We picked a fight with Black?" I pressed the ice pack he handed to me on my face.

"Not *we*. You," Jake said.

"Things just get better and better." A new wave of nausea flowed over me as it came back to me.

"That's one mean son of a bitch." Joe added.

"What the hell happened, anyway?" Jake asked Joe. "All I remember is you telling me to get Alex the hell out of there while the rest of the guys ran the gauntlet so we could leave."

"It happened fast." Joe said. "I didn't realize a guy could get his nose broken twice in the same day." He laughed at Jake.

I sat on the bed with my head in my hands. I remembered everything now. Black had come into the bar. I was sitting at the corner table with Jake, Joe and six other men. By that time I'd had enough drinks that I'd have been comfortable sitting in the middle of a fire. Black's appearance at the door worked to focus all of my attention.

The look of disapproval on his face at seeing me with those men was satisfying. It was as if I was finally proving to him what I really was.

All he did was point a finger at me and then pointed it out the door. I'd started to comply but when I reached him, he took a hold of me by my arm.

I wrenched myself away from him and growled, "Don't touch me."

"Enough," he said.

By then, the men at the table had moved to encircle us. Black maneuvered me out the door and placed himself between me and the men I'd been sitting with.

"The lady told you not to touch her," I heard one of them say.

"Stay out of this." Black's deep voice would have intimidated most men.

"You," he directed at me. "Car. Now!"

I would have followed his orders just like I always did but I heard another man say, "Who the hell are you? Her keeper?"

"Jake," Black said. "Rein in your crew. I'm taking Grey home. Let's not make more of this than we have to."

"No. Black. I'm not going." I tried to walk past him back into the bar. He scooped me up by my waist as if I weighed nothing and started to back away from the men now advancing on us.

"Drop the girl, Black." This statement was met with laughter.

"Black. Put her down." Jake approached us and hit the ground as soon as he was within Black's reach.

Before he could recover, the rest of the men swarmed Black. Most of them were on the ground before they reached me, but eventually they overwhelmed him, wrestled me away from him, and kept Black busy while Jake and Joe escorted me away.

"You better be worth the trouble," Joe brought me back. "I just got back from bailing the guys out of jail. Chris is the one you really need to make nice with though. He got a broken arm for his trouble."

Just then White's phone vibrated in my back pocket, making me jump. I pulled it out and turned it over in my hands until it quit vibrating.

"Who was that?" Jake leaned forward in his chair.

"No one I want to talk to." I put the phone back in my pocket. "Is Black okay?" I asked.

"Ha. Is Black okay?" Joe scoffed. "He's probably the only one, besides me, who walked away without a scratch. Is Black okay?" Again, he laughed.

Joe looked at Jake. "You're lucky this happened during a recruit or Posner would make you work with that face. But, he asked me to tell you to take the week to recover, then you can start training Alex to be an instructor. Until then, you can take the time to get her acquainted with the facility. Just don't let the paying customers see you like this."

Within a week, I knew that particular Mesa facility inside and out. I could have worked the desk, fixed the elevator, or cooked the daily meals if I needed to. Jake and I still had black eyes, but the swelling was gone and I was allowed to shadow him for another week before I was given my own class.

I always started my class by showing the participants my ability. I'm sure a lot of the men didn't even consider my sex but I knew there was at least one in each crowd who would have jumped at the chance to give me grief just because I was a woman and outside my range of perceived expertise. Showing each group that I knew what I was doing before the issue cropped up seemed to work best for me.

After what happened in the bar I decided hanging out at the facility might not be a bad idea. White's phone still rang at regular intervals every day. I was tempted, more than once, to answer it to find out what White had to say. I wanted to apologize for not leaving the bar with Black, apologize for getting him involved with that mess. But, then I was constantly reminded of how I'd screwed up so many times, and I couldn't bear to hear what White might say. It was over. My dad had even cut me off because of my ineptitude.

Jake and I had gotten into a routine. We'd each teach our classes, meet for lunch, finish off the day with more classes and meet for dinner. Then we'd meet in either his suite or mine and spend the night watching television, chatting or both. I kept my distance from the rest of the men who stayed at the facility. No one attempted to approach me either. Eventually, Jake started going back out on real jobs and I ached to get back out there, too. Instead, I kept teaching classes for what seemed like forever. But, having no end in sight was starting to rub on me.

Finally, I cornered Jake one night after dinner.

"Jake. I can't keep teaching these classes. It's the same thing every day, and I'm not into repetition."

"I can't help you, Alex. You have to wait until Posner gives the okay for you to do something else."

"I'm not going to wait any more. I haven't complained yet. It's been two months of nothing but classes and hanging out in my suite or yours."

"I'm sure he'll get around to it one of these days. Be patient."

"No. I'm done. I really appreciate all you've done for me, but I'm done. I *need* to get outta here. The only thing I have to look forward to is getting with you after work in your suite or mine. How sad is that?"

"Pretty sad." He smiled as if he'd accomplished something.

"I'll stay till the end of the week."

"Promise you'll finish out the week?"

"Yeah. It's only two more days. I think I can handle it."

"What are you going to do?"

"I have no idea. Fall off the grid. Move to Alaska and live off the land. Go to some foreign country and turn myself in for crimes against the state. I don't know." If only he knew how serious I was about the last statement he might decide to buy my plane ticket to Romania.

The next morning at breakfast, Jake took me aside and led me back to the main office.

"Ms. Grey." An older gentleman stood from the office chair and came around the desk to shake my hand. He looked somehow familiar, but I was certain I'd never seen him before.

I took his hand. His grip was firm and brief.

"Sir." I assumed I was speaking to my current boss, Mark Posner.

"Sit, please." He motioned to a chair as he sat on the corner of the desk. Jake held back near the door.

"Jake here tells me we are going to lose you if I don't switch out your jobs."

"Yes, sir. I plan to finish out the week."

"What makes you think you can pressure me into what you want?" He raised his eyebrows and his look became almost sinister.

"Sir? That was not my intention. I was just stating a fact." I stood from my chair.

Who the hell did this guy think he was?

"I had every intention of staying until the end of the week. However, I am prepared to leave you to your facility effective immediately. I'm not cut out for teaching classes in the same place all day, every day. It's a waste of my time, and your resources. I don't *need* a job. Least of all a job that's a waste of my expertise." I held out my hand. "I appreciate you allowing me to kill some time teaching at your facility."

He looked me up and down. "Put your hand down, Ms. Grey. You have more balls than most men. I was prepared to accept your apology, but I see you aren't the type to be—"

"Bullied, sir?" I finished his sentence. "Not at all, sir." I gave him a sterile smile.

"Maybe you are cut out for more than I thought you were. What is it you'd like to do, Ms. Grey?"

"I'm game for most everything except contract hits."

"Everything *except* contract hits?" He laughed. "Do you think we do that kind of thing around here?"

"I have no idea, sir, and I don't want to know. Just know I won't do them."

"Have you performed that service in the past?" His look became amused.

"You won't find it on my resume, sir."

The room was quiet for a full minute as Posner walked back behind the desk and took his seat.

"Would you be interested in a retrieval mission?"

"Depends, sir."

"So it would." He took in a deep breath. "I need someone to retrieve payment from a former client. Do you think you could do this?"

"It's highly likely. Will I have a crew or will I be doing this alone?"

"Alone? No, Ms. Grey. I'll send *you* with Jake and *his* crew."

"That's acceptable to me, sir."

"Are you sure? You seem to have a problem with authority."

"No problem with authority, just a problem with waste, mismanagement, and stupidity, sir."

"Don't start stepping on those big balls of yours, Ms. Grey."

"Of course not, sir."

"Jake'll fill you in on all the details." He dismissed me.

ONCE JAKE AND I GOT a sufficient distance from the office, he stepped in front of me and backed me into the wall with his advance.

"What the hell was that?"

"What do you mean?" I wasn't comfortable with him in my face like this.

"Posner isn't a guy to play with. Don't piss him off."

"I won't kiss anyone's ass. I refuse."

"If there was anyone's ass you need to kiss, it's Posner's."

I laughed.

"I'm serious, Alex. He's not someone to take lightly. Piss him off and things can go bad."

"I seriously doubt Posner cares if I quit working as an instructor at his facility. That position is easy enough to fill."

"Maybe not if that's all you were. Posner called you in because he doesn't want you working anywhere else. That much is obvious."

"He has no choice who I work for, Jake." I glared.

"You'd be surprised."

"You might be surprised, yourself."

He backed away, and the two of us made our way back to his suite where he gave me a short briefing of the job.

Chapter Eight

THE STREETS WERE QUIET AND dark. None of the street
lights were working. I assumed that meant the people
who lived here didn't want their after dark behavior to be
observed.

"You ready for this?" Jake asked as we pulled up to the
curb.

"Yep. You?" I looked in the side-view mirror and watched
as the rest of the crew pulled up behind us.

"Let's go." He put the car in park and shut off the engine.

I stood in full view of the peephole and Jake stood with his
back to the wall near the door so he'd not be seen. I knocked.

"Look lost," Jake ordered under his breath as he stood
with his back to the wall beside the door. The two other men
had worked their way to the back door.

I heard the deadbolt being unlocked, and tensed.

"Yes?" I heard a man ask through the small crack in the door.

"I'm sorry. My car broke down, and I was hoping you'd let me use your phone?"

"Sure."

The target slid the chain lock and I fidgeted until he opened the door wide enough for me to step in. I smiled and stepped passed him and into the house. As he was shutting the door, Jake muscled his way in.

"What the hell is going on?" The target tried to throw a punch Jake's direction.

I grabbed his arms and pulled them behind him.

"Wanna let the rest of the guys in?" I asked Jake.

"You got him?"

"Yep." I pinched the pressure point on his neck and he went to his knees. His ball cap fell to the floor and skittered across the dull hardwood.

Jake stepped past us to let the other men in the back door and I pulled out my pistol.

"Let's go find a seat, shall we?"

"What the hell is going on?" he demanded again.

"You'll have to talk to my boss. I'm just the muscle," I said as I pushed him toward his table. "Sit. Hands flat on the table," I ordered as Jake, Eric and Joe joined us.

"Jake. Dude," the target said then. "I didn't recognize you earlier. We can work this out."

"The last two times I've been here to work this out you didn't answer the door. Here's how we're going to work this out. You pay cash now or I'm calling a moving van and we'll do a little house cleaning. We'll take everything, especially the dust. Any cash we find in this sweep goes to our cleaning fees. You'll still owe."

"I don't have it, man. I swear."

Jake nodded at Eric who turned around and made a call from his cell.

"Start searching, Joe," Jake said. "You've got maybe fifteen minutes before the movers show. Any drugs you find need to come back to me, here." He pointed to the table.

"You got it," Joe said and headed out of the room.

"Man. Don't do this. If you take those drugs I'll never get you the money and they'll kill me."

"Your problem. Trying to screw your current contact by trying to get a better price elsewhere when you've already promised the shipment is *never* good for your health."

"How'd you know that?"

"Why else haven't you made your sale? Not just that, you weren't upfront about the cargo. You turned us into drug smugglers."

"No one knows you guys helped me out. I swear it."

"Posner knows. He knows you used his company to smuggle drugs and now *you* know he won't stand for it."

"Man. Please. Don't take my stash. All I have to do is schedule a meeting. Then I'll have Posner's money, I swear it."

Jake shook his head. "Where's the stash?" He chambered a round and pointed his pistol at the target.

The man cringed.

"Hands on the table!" I chambered a round of my own.

"It's in the couch, man." He was visibly shaking.

"Joe. Check the couch!" Jake hollered as he holstered his weapon again. I kept my pistol at the ready and pointed at the target. It gave me a sense of security. Jake hadn't told me drugs were involved, and what the hell did we want with drugs, anyway.

We waited for Joe to respond and I wondered what the hell I'd gotten myself into. I was in the house of a drug dealer and we weren't trying to get him arrested. We were just trying to find his stash and take his money.

At this point, I had no choice but to remain exactly where I was, doing exactly what I was doing. This was more than a little sketchy and I didn't know if we were the good guys or the bad guys.

Joe walked toward us and dropped a large plastic bag of white powder onto the table. "The couch is full of it."

"See. That wasn't so hard, now was it?" Jake told the man. "Eric, you can call off the movers."

"Jake, you can't take it," Danny pleaded.

"What do I want with drugs? If I take it, all I have to do is dispose of it. We aren't drug dealers *or* drug smugglers. Oh, wait. Yes we are. Because of you. This isn't the first time you've pulled this bullshit, Danny. But, it is the last."

"Yes. I swear. I'll never do it again." He held up shaking hands in a gesture of surrender.

"Hands flat on the table!" I reminded him.

"Here's what's going to happen, Danny. First, you're going to call your contact and schedule a meet in about an hour. Then, you're going to get up and clean out that couch and move the contents to the back of that Dodge Durango parked out on the street. You'll do the deal, get your cash, and we'll take our cut."

"Okay. That's fair, man. My phone is on the coffee table." He pointed.

"Damn it! Hands on the table!" I smacked him in the back of the head hard.

"Ow! Shit!" He reached toward the back of his head so I grabbed him by the hair with my free hand and pushed his face onto the table.

"Hands on the table," I said into his ear with the muzzle of my gun pressing into his side.

The men all gave me looks of approval as Danny was allowed to make his call. With that one small gesture, I'd won their respect, for the moment.

Jake made him use the speaker phone on the cell for the call. Danny had to practically beg to get his meeting set up before tomorrow. But, he told his contact that he had some bills that had to be paid before the day was done. I suppose they'd found themselves in similar situations because they finally agreed.

"Good. Get it loaded up." Jake told him after Danny had hung up the phone.

Eric and Joe followed him to the couch and tore it wide open, exposing nothing but the white plastic bags. Danny bent down, grabbed an armload, and walked toward the door. Eric followed him out and Joe remained near the front door, weapon in hand.

"WE'RE GOING TO DO A drug deal?" I asked Jake as we watched Danny hauling the packages to the SUV.

"No. Danny is. We're just going to be there to take our cut when the deal is done."

I still wasn't sure how I felt about this. We should be turning his ass in and keeping the drugs off the streets. But, I knew now that not everything in life was black and white, good and bad. The concept of Helix and his gray hat status was much more clear to me. Maybe that's what he'd been alluding to when he seemed surprised I was going from White and Associates to Mesa. One was a gray hat operation and the other was a white hat operation.

Besides, it sounded as if this Danny guy had deceived Posner's guys into helping him smuggle drugs. What else could Mesa do, now that they'd helped him bring drugs into the country? About all they really could do was get their money and get as far away as quickly as they could.

Eric and Joe kept Danny moving at a steady pace until the SUV was loaded.

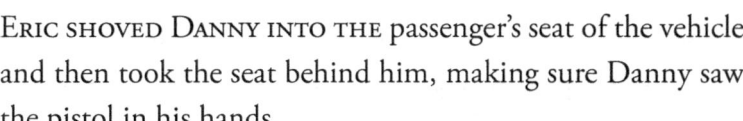

ERIC SHOVED DANNY INTO THE passenger's seat of the vehicle and then took the seat behind him, making sure Danny saw the pistol in his hands.

Jake tossed Joe his car keys. They shared a nod and Jake got behind the wheel of the Durango.

"Let's go." Joe told me as he walked to the Charger. We sped off in the direction of the meet before the other vehicle was even running.

Two blocks before the chosen address, Joe turned into an alley and parked the car. He got out, so I followed.

He was pulling a rifle from the trunk.

"Here." He handed it to me and pulled out another one.

"What's this for?"

"We're Jake and Eric's protection. You take this roof and I'll take that one." He pointed.

The chosen meeting place was a midsized city park with plenty of darkened areas. From my rooftop I could see Joe setting up and I did the same. I placed my rifle on the edge of the rooftop so I could see as much of the park as possible. When I looked through the scope I realized it had an infrared setting. That would come in handy if they met under the trees.

Within five minutes Jake, Eric and Danny pulled into the parking lot. The three of them stepped to the back of the vehicle and waited.

About ten minutes of watching Danny pace in front of Jake and Eric, who stood at the two back corners of the vehicle, was enough for me. Thankfully, an identical Durango to the company vehicle pulled into the lot. They parked five parking spots away. Three men exited that vehicle as well.

Danny and one of the men from the other vehicle met in the middle. A short exchange of words had the man following Danny to the back of our SUV. Eric opened the liftgate and the new man did a quick inspection. He gave Danny a nod of approval and the two of them walked back to the middle ground where one of the other men had brought forward a briefcase.

He placed the case on the ground and backed away a step. Danny had the moves memorized and waited for the men to move back before he opened the case.

More nods of approval led to all six men meeting in the middle of the lot where sets of keys were exchanged. I didn't realize what was going on until I saw the three drug dealers enter our Durango and drive off, leaving the other SUV in our possession.

Jake held out his hand and Danny willingly gave up the briefcase. The three of them walked to the SUV where Jake inspected the cash as well. It was too dark to see what was being said, but it obviously irritated Danny. He started pointing his finger into Jake's chest and then made a grab for Jake's gun.

Eric had already gotten into the passenger's seat and was looking straight forward. *Why wasn't he getting out to help his partner?*

I watched as Danny and Jake scuffled. Danny got control of Jake's 9mm and leveled it on Jake, who stood there as if he were merely annoyed and not in fear for his life.

I could tell Danny was making some kind of demands because he kept pointing at the ground in front of himself with his free hand. Jake only slowly shook his head and crossed his arms. Still, Eric wasn't getting out of the vehicle, but at least he was turned around in his seat with his weapon pointed at Danny.

The argument went on for two full minutes and the only change in the scene was how irritated Danny became. I caught a few words in the darkness. Danny repeatedly said *mine, now,* and the f-word, but Jake only said one word, *no.* He stood there, stoic and unmoved.

I waited as long as I could, but when Danny slipped his finger onto the trigger I pressed down on my own. I barely noticed the pop of the rifle or felt the kick. I was focused on Danny. He hit the ground and the only movement was the blood pooling around him. I watched Jake retrieve his 9mm and get into the SUV. As soon as he was inside the vehicle I picked up my weapon and made my way to the edge of the building. Joe was still looking through his scope when I reached the fire escape.

"Let's go. Now!" I hollered across to him.

He jumped up and followed my instructions without question.

We met at the car, placed our rifles back into the trunk, and sped back to the Mesa facility. The only words exchanged during the drive came from Joe. Shortly after we got onto the main road he said, "Nice shot."

I worked the scenario over and over in my head. There had been no other outcome, except for one. Eric. He hadn't taken the shot. I hated that I didn't know more about what was going on down there, but his hesitance made me wonder if my shot was completely necessary.

Joe pulled directly up to the front doors of the facility.

"Go ahead and go in. I'm going to put the equipment away," he said.

I stepped out of the Charger and took a seat in the waiting area. The man at the front desk only gave me a nod and then went back to his business.

Joe joined me before Jake and Eric pulled in.

"They'll be here soon." He took a seat in the chair across from me.

I nodded.

"I have to admit I didn't think you had it in you. Your first is always the hardest."

His assumption that this was my first kill made me giggle, but it wasn't out of glee. I put my hand to my forehead and rubbed. Suddenly I had a terrible headache.

A few deep breaths helped. I put my hand back in my lap and looked him directly in the face. "This isn't my first."

"Then why look so depressed?"

"I used to ask the questions before pulling the trigger, but now the questions come after I've pulled the trigger."

"No need to worry about this one. You saved Jake. I would have taken the shot, but I didn't have the best line of sight."

I sighed and shook my head.

"It's best to check your conscience at the door with this job, Alex."

I didn't respond. The two of us sat in silence for more than half an hour. Finally Jake and Eric came in the door carrying the briefcase. Joe and I stood to greet them.

"Thanks, man." Jake held his hand out for Joe.

"Not me," Joe said and hiked his head my direction.

"*You* saved my ass out there?" Jake directed at me.

"Don't sound so surprised. What do you think I was trained for at White and Associates? I didn't do windows, answer the phone or file things."

"Sorry. It's easy to forget your reputation." He clapped me on the shoulder. "Let's get this to Posner and do the debriefing."

We followed Jake back to Posner's office. I didn't think he'd be here at this time of night. Maybe it was because he was waiting to hear about the job.

"Ah. Thank you, Jake."

Posner walked around his desk and took the briefcase from Jake. He then returned to his desk, opened the case, and flipped through the cash.

"This looks right. Anything happen I should know about?"

"Yes. Danny managed to take my weapon and Alex took Danny out. I called in a cleaning team, so everything is taken care of," Jake replied. This was nothing like the debriefing at White and Associates. We were expected to practically write a full detailed report. This was much less formal.

Posner's eyebrows raised as he looked at me. "I thought you said you wouldn't kill anyone."

"I didn't say that, sir. I said I would not accept contract hits. However, I'm not opposed to protecting my teammates."

"That's a definite plus."

His tone was condescending. If I hadn't already made up my mind that I didn't like Posner this short conversation would have solidified my dislike.

JAKE SHOWED UP IN MY room a few minutes after I'd gotten comfortable in front of my TV for the night.

"What's up?" I asked when I opened the door to let him in.

"Not much, but I have a job I'd like to talk to you about."

"Sounds good. What's the job?"

"We do this job every year and it lasts three months. I have to make sure you're up for it. Are you up for being unreachable for three months?"

"Who'd try to reach me?"

"White. He should be calling—"

My phone vibrated in my back pocket and I pulled it out to decline the call. "How'd you know it was White?"

"It's White and Associates' office number on the caller ID," he said.

"Have you been spying on me?"

"Not intentionally. I happened to see the number, that's all."

I sighed. "Yeah, it's White. I don't want to talk to him, though."

"So get rid of the phone."

"I can't. I mean, I could. I'm just not ready to."

"So it wasn't Black you had the affair with." Jake smiled as if he'd completed a mission with flying colors.

"No. It wasn't Black. And yes, I'm an idiot."

"Maybe we can cure you of your addiction." He pointed to the phone I still held in my hands.

"Yeah."

I walked to the side table near my bed and put the phone in the top drawer. I felt naked. This was the first time I'd not had the phone in my pocket or my hands for months.

"So, it's settled." Jake said, taking a seat in my sitting room and picking up the TV remote control. "You'll come down to South America with us."

"Yep."

The two of us sat on the couch for about half an hour before Eric showed up at my door with a bottle of Jack and Joe followed him in with ice and cola.

"Hey! You're coming along, aren't you?" Eric asked me.

"Yes."

"Great! Let's celebrate."

He'd already made his way to my kitchenette area and was pulling glasses down from the cupboards. Joe started filling the glasses with ice and Eric followed behind him with the booze and poured in generous amounts before Joe topped them off with cola.

"Jack coke is what you were drinking at the bar and since you're the new guy we thought it would be appropriate," Joe said as he handed me my glass.

"Thanks." I hadn't planned on drinking tonight, but I might as well. I had nothing else to do. I could tell I wasn't getting rid of these guys any time soon.

Somehow, the four of us fit on the small couch in front of my television. I was practically sitting on Jake's lap, though.

They each took their turn congratulating me on taking out Danny and protecting Jake's ass. Jake even gave my knee a squeeze when he thanked me again for taking the shot. For some reason, it all made me feel better about everything. I was starting to look forward to doing more jobs with these men.

After their praise we moved onto talking about the job in South America. All we needed to do was guard an oil refinery for three months and then our replacements would show up. But, something I was to be included in on was an annual ritual these three men shared.

We'd hire a river boat and slowly float down the Amazon to the refinery, fishing and drinking all the way there. Then we'd meet up with the rest of the security crew. It actually sounded like fun.

The four of us eventually chose a television show and Eric kept all of our drinks full. It didn't take long for me to drift off into my thoughts and tune out the television as well as the men.

I found myself back in Romania watching Vasile strutting around in his birthday suit. The appreciative feelings I'd had before came back even stronger and I found myself on his bed with him looking down at me with lustful eyes. Being with Vasile was enjoyable but the moment was missing something until I pulled out my knife and stabbed him in the neck. His blood was warm as it poured over me. The feeling of complete satisfaction turned to utter disgust. I yelled "No," and pushed Vasile away from me before I realized my reoccurring dream had found its way back into my nighttime schedule after a month of dreamless nights.

It hadn't been Vasile I was pushing away. I had fallen asleep on my couch and Jake was still sitting next to me. It was him I'd pushed away.

"What's wrong? You're shaking." He'd pulled me close to him and his voice was reassuring.

"Bad dream." I wanted to pull away from him, and tried. His grip was strong and so was his scent.

"What is it?"

I just shook my head and tried to get my breathing under control.

"I'm here," he said, smoothing my hair.

His strong grip, heady scent, and comforting manner made me shake even harder until I finally started to cry. Crying was the last thing I wanted to do.

"Is it Danny?"

Again, I just shook my head as he held me tighter. He didn't say anything else until I'd controlled my sobbing.

"I'm so sorry, Jake." I sniffed and got up for some tissues.

"Is it White?" he asked.

I laughed at that one. "No."

"Do you want to talk about it?"

"No." I blew my nose, threw the tissue in the trash can, and sat at the opposite side of the couch.

Jake slid in close again and put his arms around my shoulders and I let him. His persistence and warmth soothed me. I knew the alcohol played a large part in my acceptance of his attentions and I didn't care. I didn't know what I'd do if he wanted to take it further later, but I needed this right now. I let myself fall asleep in his arms.

Chapter Nine

I WOKE UP TO A TERRIBLE cramp in my neck. I groaned as I sat up and woke Jake, who'd been snoring.

"Morning," he said while rubbing the back of his own neck. "Next time, we're moving to the bed."

I felt my face flush and my stomach protested the thought.

Jake let out a laugh.

"What's so funny?"

The shrillness in my voice hurt my head.

"Not that I don't find you attractive, but sex with *you* is the last thing on my mind," he said.

"Is that so?" I caught myself straightening my hairdo. "What the hell is wrong with having sex with me?"

Jake laughed again.

"Hey, if you insist—" He started to lift his shirt as a threat.

"No!" I reached over and pulled his shirt back down.

"You're too easy. Who would have thought a woman in your position would be such a prude?"

"I am not a prude," I objected.

"Okay."

His tone clearly said he didn't believe me, but he started to lift his shirt again.

He lifted it slowly and stopped just above his stomach. His abs were a welcome sight. I got lost in the vision for only a split second before I told him, "Put your shirt down, Jake. We are not going to have sex."

"Hey. I'm willing to sacrifice a little if it'll make you happy."

He still hadn't lowered his shirt.

I fought with myself. My head cocked to the side, but the indignant remark didn't form. Instead, I licked my lips, used the angry nostril flare in a mock show of excitement, and took a deep breath.

"Sacrifice? Really? You'd do that for me?"

He'd pissed me off, but I hoped I hid that fact with my raised eyebrows, forced smile, and teasing tone of voice. He'd learn to feel privileged to even have unspoken fantasies.

I lifted my own shirt as I walked closer to him. His eyes bulged somewhat. I timed removing my shirt just right. I lifted it up over my head just as I reached him. He hurried to get his own off.

Jake stood in front of me, shirtless. It was a nice sight and I considered, only for a fleeting second, taking it further.

The appreciation and hunger in his eyes as he took in the vision of me in just my bra almost made me cave. I regained control as soon as my mind flitted to White's face the first time he saw me in this position. White's eyes had carried more. The vision of me in a vulnerable position meant more to White than it did to Jake. They both held the hunger deep inside their eyes, but White's hunger was muted by respect for the situation.

I looked down at myself in a self-conscious move.

At least I'm wearing my cute bra.

It was a bra I'd bought in the hopes of showing off. It accented and supported. Somehow, seeing what Jake was seeing gave me the strength to look him in the face again. I wouldn't share myself with anyone who didn't look at me the way White had. The man would have to realize, before we had sex, how lucky he really was.

I trailed my finger across his chest and watched as he took a couple deep breaths before I hauled back and slugged him hard in the stomach.

He doubled over and tried to catch his breath while I put my shirt back on.

"Still think I'm a prude?" I asked.

"Yes," he squeezed out.

"Asshole."

He made his way back to the couch and put his shirt back on just as his phone chirped.

"Yeah, boss," was all I heard before I closed the bathroom door. I needed to brush my teeth and shower.

I EXPECTED JAKE TO BE gone when I came out, but I'd still dried and dressed in the bathroom, just in case. As it turned out, Jake was still in my room when I exited the bathroom.

"We've got a job."

"Okay?"

"This is a serious job. I have to know you're up for it. If you don't think you can handle it, tell me right away, okay?"

"Well, what is it?"

"It's over in Sudan."

"Africa?"

"Yep. One of our crews has run into some trouble. We need to get our asses over there right away and help out. Our guys have been guarding a politician over there and all hell's broke loose. Now they are hoping to get their charge to a small village in Sudan sometime tomorrow. If we leave right now we'll be able to meet them there and escort everyone back to the airport." He took a breath. "There could be some resistance. Have you ever seen any combat?"

"Not really."

"Well, I think you'd be okay and you'll be with me. All you need to do is follow orders and follow my lead. Think you can do it?"

"Yeah. Who's the politician?"

"I don't know."

"What do you mean? How can you not know?"

"I don't need to know."

"I don't understand how you work this way."

I shook my head.

"Why do we need to know?"

"What if he's a terrible person?"

"What does that have to do with it? Don't forget, our main goal, after they get him to his little village, is to get our guys home." .

"Can you find out who it is so I can look into it?"

I'd been burned by not doing my due diligence before and I didn't want to repeat it.

"No, Alex. You either work this job with me or you don't. I don't know the reason behind your compulsion to know all the details. We provide a service and we get paid for it. Simple as that. So, make your decision. Do you want to help me provide a service and get a paycheck or do you want to sit this one out?"

He'd put me in a tight spot. It wasn't a hit, it was mostly retrieval detail. So what was I hedging for?

"Okay. I'm with you."

"Good. We leave right now. Get packed."

I grabbed up my forever-ready pack that sat near the door.

"Ready."

Jake smiled and gestured for me to follow him. We stopped by his room long enough for him to grab up his own ready-made pack. Then we rounded up Joe and Eric. The four of us were joined by six more men. We were driven in a van to the airport where we boarded a light passenger jet.

I entered directly behind Jake, who was the first on the plane.

"Sit with me," he said as he patted the seat next to him.

Joe and Eric came in next and took the two seats across the aisle from us. I watched as the rest of the men filed in. The mood was light and remained that way as we taxied out onto the runway and lifted off.

When we were up in the air one of the men moved up toward us.

"What'll you have, Jake?"

"Make it a beer, Stan. Oh, mix Ms. Grey a Jack cola, please," he added when Stan took Eric and Joe's drink order.

I looked at Jake in shock. We were on our way to a possible fire fight and they were going to be drinking?

He must have read my face because he said, "What? It's a twenty-hour flight. I don't know about you, but I could use a little something to cut the tension and help me sleep before we get there."

"Fine," I said. "Stan, make mine a straight shot with a cola back, please."

"Of course," he replied with a broad grin.

A couple of the men grumbled that Stan didn't offer to mix their drinks or bring them beer after he served us, but were still smiling when they moved to the front of the plane to serve themselves.

The flight was a mixture of men playing cards, chatting, joking and snoring. I even found myself waking up from a good six hours of sleep right before we landed in Sudan.

When we exited the airplane we were led directly to a couple of Hummers that drove us over dry roads, creating a dust storm behind us.

After several hours of being jostled around inside the vehicle, we arrived at a small village with small, roughly built wooden houses. There was no welcoming committee. In fact, the brightly dressed women grabbed up their children or ushered them into the small buildings as we drove by.

When we stepped out of our vehicles in the middle of town an elderly man came forward and addressed our party with obvious concern. As soon as he approached us, people started gathering. He spoke perfect English, but everyone around us was speaking in Arabic.

Jake explained to him that we were in his village to protect Malik Abu Ibrahim.

He'd led me to believe he didn't even know the guy's name. I decided not to get too mad. We were in a hurry to get here and we didn't have time for me to do any research.

The old man laughed. It was a sour laugh devoid of mirth.

"Yes, Malik Abu Ibrahim. His family lives there." He pointed directly off to his left without looking.

I followed his gesture until I saw a building and a woman with a small boy. She looked terrified as did the rest of the village.

"We had hoped to never see him again. Instead, he brings back trouble."

He indicated our weapons.

The old man shouted something in Arabic at the gathering crowd and I heard our charge's name in there. He pointed with venom to the woman and her child. The scowls we were given made it obvious none of them were happy we were here or that Ibrahim was returning to his home. The crowd dispersed quickly.

We weren't given any offers of a place to stay, so Jake turned us toward the house with the woman and small child to seek refuge.

He approached her.

"Do you speak English?"

The only response the woman gave was to cower over her child protectively.

Jake tried to explain what was going on, but it was obvious she didn't understand. Instead, he called over one of the men and told him to explain it to her.

"I think you should know that the old man told everyone to leave the village," the man said as he came up to Jake and the woman.

"That's good. I'd rather not have an entire village to worry about," Jake replied.

"I think they plan to leave her and her child behind."

"Damn it. I'll go talk to their spokesman and see if I can arrange a way out for them, as well."

Jake followed the old man after instructing us to start setting up a defensible area. At least there was no good way for anyone to sneak up on us. We could see for miles in every direction.

I helped fill sandbags with dirt for a good half an hour before I saw dust rising up in the distance.

"Joe," I got his attention and nodded in the direction of the tan smudge on the horizon.

"Go get Jake," Joe told me.

It didn't take me long to find him. He was handing the old man a wad of cash.

"Jake." I interrupted the transaction.

He turned around. "What is it?"

"There are vehicles coming down the road."

"That'll be our guys escorting Ibrahim, I hope."

"Send the woman and her child here. We need to leave now," the old man said before he went into his own home.

Jake led me back to our small band of men.

He asked Eric, who held a pair of binoculars to his eyes, "Our guys?"

"Looks that way, but I think they have company."

"Already? Shit. How long do you think we have?"

"Maybe fifteen minutes, if they make it."

Jake started issuing orders immediately. He sent the man who spoke Arabic to hurry the woman out of her home and let the village elder know they had to go now or risk being caught in the crossfire.

He had three of us filling sandbags as fast as we could, three more building bunkers in front of the vehicles they'd parked to block the road and against the front row of houses near the road. Eric remained glued to his binoculars and Joe was dispersing weapons and ammo into the bunkers.

As the stain of dust approached I felt my adrenaline level rise. My heart started to beat harder and my breath became more shallow.

"Relax. Use up all your reserves now and you'll be exhausted before the fight really begins," Jake warned as he came up behind me. "You're probably the best shot on the line. I need you to get up on this roof and start picking off as many as you can as soon as they get into range."

"Our guys are ahead of the trucks a good distance, so you'll have time to get adjusted," Eric said as he pulled a gorgeous Barrett .50 caliber out of the back of one of the vehicles.

"This is a single-shot bolt action rifle. Think you can handle her?"

I felt a sense of security as I reached for the rifle.

"This is my girl," I said, thinking about my own Barrett back in the closet at White and Associates.

"What?"

"I had to give up my Barrett when I left White and Associates. She looks just like my baby back home."

"No shit?"

"No shit."

I reached again for the rifle.

"Then you should have no troubles, unless you never get on that damn roof. Get your ass up there and I'll hand her up to you."

Chapter Ten

"**D**ON'T FALL THROUGH," ERIC CALLED up to me as he took his position behind the sandbags piled in front of the small house I was perched on.

I'd worried about that as soon as I got up on the roof and heard the creaking of the boards. I managed to find a good position at the peak and positioned the rifle just over the edge. I only hoped the kick of the weapon didn't push me off backwards.

I'd made the men hand me some boards and had quickly nailed them to the roof to give me some holding power for my feet.

I looked through my scope and saw our guys speeding our direction. No one was manning the turrets of the Humvees, but the two small trucks trying to catch our guys were full of armed men taking turns firing ineffective rounds at the armored vehicles.

"There's about twenty of them," I called down as I chambered a round.

I gave the rungs a quick kick to test their security. They held. I fired. A man slumped over into the bed of the truck.

As always, the kick was strong and welcomed. I let it push me down somewhat, using my legs like springs. I wouldn't be able to fire as fast as I hoped with this setup, but I could still get the job done.

I chambered another round.

The man in the back of the truck was a test shot. This time I aimed for the driver.

I fired, recoiled with my legs, pushed myself back into position in time to see the vehicle swerve off the road and flip into the air. Men flew out of the bed of the vehicle and skittered across the ground. The second pickup truck fishtailed as it tried to miss the falling men.

I chambered another round and targeted the next driver.

The first vehicle touched down and slid several feet creating a huge dust cloud, obscuring the second truckload of armed men.

Two seconds later the remaining vehicle sped through the tan cloud.

I heard Eric's voice below me but didn't let the words seep into my conscious thought. The second driver was in my sights.

I squeezed the trigger and could practically see the bullet's path as it made its way to the target.

I chambered another round and watched the bullet slice through the driver. Men started to emerge from the settling dust near the first transport, their weapons drawn.

Another squeeze of the trigger and a man fell out of the back of the truck rolling to a stop.

The sound of gunfire, other than mine, reached my ears.

The two Humvees that carried our men slid into place alongside the two we had used to block the road. Men streamed out of them and took cover inside the hurriedly constructed sandbag bunkers.

The dust had dissipated and the men who were left from the truck that had flipped were running toward the other truck for cover. The second truck had rolled to a stop and all of the men were out of the back of the vehicle and targeting us.

I chambered my last round in the cartridge and fired.

My target dropped, but it hadn't been my round that took him out. I knew it hadn't been me because the timing was off and the damage wasn't anywhere near a .50 caliber round.

I growled.

"My fucking target, asshole!" I had no idea who I was screaming at, but I didn't like wasting bullets.

I slid down the backside of the roof for cover while I changed out my cartridge.

When I emerged, the remaining hostiles had dwindled and were all behind the vehicle for protection.

I fired and my round ripped through the side of the truck. I smiled when I saw three men fall backwards.

I heard another .50 caliber firing and watched the vehicle being torn to shreds. One of our guys had finally manned the turret of one of the Humvees.

It was over before it even started and my fingers itched. I scanned the wreckage for movement. There was none.

The silence was a warm, comfortable blanket for a full minute, then it started to become suffocating.

Someone besides Jake barked orders just before we all drowned in the quiet. "Team two! Clean up! The rest of you, stand fast!"

I was in the best position to take out a threat that may be playing dead. My sights touched every body as the group of three men fanned out and started checking pulses.

Movement.

A man near the flipped truck grabbed a weapon and rolled behind the truck.

My elevated position allowed me to see over the vehicle, and the man, though he thought he was safe for the moment, was mostly exposed.

I fired.

Threat eliminated.

The men who stood below me brought their weapons into firing positions in response to my latest round. The sound of my .50 caliber had elicited more movement directly in front of the middle man of team two.

His response was quick and sharp.

The team moved a little quicker after that. They stopped checking pulses and simply put one in the head of each of the bodies. The repeated pops made me flinch. It occurred to me that it was one thing to put down a threat and quite another to just put them down.

But, if they don't do it, they'll just turn into threats later. It's not like we have the capability to take prisoners. I tried to rationalize it.

I remained on my perch until the team returned to the village and probably would have stayed there all night had Eric not demanded I give up the Barrett.

Reluctantly, I handed it down to him. Then I allowed Joe to help me climb down.

I dangled my feet over the edge and waited for Joe to grab my legs. When he had a good grip, I let myself slide through his arms to the ground.

"Impressive," Joe said into my ear as my feet touched the ground.

"That's the second time you've called me an asshole recently." Jake interrupted anything else Joe had planned to say.

"What?"

"Sorry about taking your target." Jake clarified his statement.

"That was you?"

He nodded and grinned.

"Asshole," I repeated. "I don't appreciate wasting rounds outside of practice."

The men who heard the exchange laughed, but I was serious.

Jake turned to the other man who'd been issuing orders since he got there.

"Lance, this is Alex Grey." Jake introduced us.

"*The* Ms. Grey?" Lance beamed as he offered his hand.

I took it and he gave me a hearty shake.

"Where's the rest of your guys?" Jake's voice had turned to all business.

"I lost two guys back at the palace. We lost the other five on the road here."

"Damn. Sorry, man." Jake clapped Lance on the shoulder.

"I know. But, we don't have time for this right now. I'm sure we've got a small army behind us. We need to get the fuck outta here."

"Better mount up, then," Jake said. "It's a good three-hour drive back to the airport."

"Should be good to go, then," Lance said. "Mount up men!"

We all complied, but I noticed our charge was nowhere to be seen.

"Where's what's-his-face?" I asked Jake.

"Our job is complete. We got him safely to his destination. If he's smart, he's already dug a hole to hide out in."

Within two minutes, we were back on the road heading back the way we came. Less than a quarter mile outside the village we came across the villagers walking back to their homes. They had a captive, tied up and being drug back to town.

"Bad decisions," Jake said.

"What's going on?"

"Our former charge thought he could take refuge in his home village, but they don't seem to care too much for him."

"Shouldn't we do something?" I asked as we passed by the mob.

"Nope. He paid us to get him here, not to protect him from his own family. I'm sure they'll hand him over."

"So what was the point?" I was flabbergasted.

"We get paid." He shrugged.

WE GET PAID.

Jake's phrase kept playing over in my mind as I bounced along in the Humvee.

We get paid.

I've always been paid, but I had a higher sense of purpose when I worked with White and Associates. Now, I was reduced to nothing but a paycheck.

The firefight, though short, had been exhilarating. Maybe it was okay to get paid for this kind of thing, even if it didn't serve any real purpose.

Still, it felt wrong.

"What's up?" Jake interrupted my thoughts with a nudge to my ribs.

"What do you mean?"

"We've been talking to you and you're just staring out the window."

"Oh. Just thinking."

"'Bout what?"

"The job."

"What'd you think of your first combat experience?"

"Not much different than anything I've done before, just did it in a group and with live ammo."

"How many did you get? I only got the one I stole from you."

"I didn't count."

That was a complete lie. I always counted. I'd fired seven rounds and took out eight men, thanks to the shrapnel from the truck. It would have been nine if Jake hadn't stolen my target.

"You did better with the Barrett than I thought you would," Eric added.

"I told you. The Barrett is my favorite."

"I thought it was going to throw you off that roof," Joe said.

"I thought it might, too," I admitted.

"Nice teamwork out there, guys," Jake said.

I guess this was the way the guys patted each other on the back when they made it out alive.

The conversations continued, but now that I'd said a few words the guys left me alone until we reached our destination.

I had to go through the same kind of pats on the back when we were joined by the rest of the Mesa crew and boarded the plane.

It was much more congested for the flight home, but that didn't stop me from sleeping for almost the full twenty hours.

Chapter Eleven

A S SOON AS WE RETURNED to the Mesa facility, we were ushered to one of the rifle shooting ranges.

I followed in line as we gathered on the field with the metal targets behind us. We were instructed to grab an empty champagne glass as we walked past a table that held the glasses and chilled bottles of champagne. The brand wasn't familiar to me.

A charter bus rolled up to the range and six scantily clad women paraded out. Posner exited the bus right behind the women and took his place in front of us. He looked like a politician about to give a speech.

He waited until he had a quiet audience.

"Good job, men. We lost seven good men, but we got the job done. You should be proud," he said.

The women, in skimpy shorts and halter tops, took their cue and started pouring the champagne into our glasses.

When everyone had a full glass, Posner lifted his for a toast.

"For our fallen comrades. You will be missed. And for those of you who came back, to more successful jobs in the future."

The men were quiet as they downed their champagne in salute and we all bowed our heads for a full sixty seconds in honor of the lost employees. Then the women started walking around refilling the glasses.

Jake, Lance, and Posner moved to stand by the bus and everyone left them alone to talk.

Thank goodness it was a short speech.

I watched Posner's lips. They were getting a major ass-chewing. At least Lance was.

"In the future be sure to only lose those who don't have families. You get me, Lance?" Posner shook his head. "I'm not looking forward to calling Jeff's wife and paying out the ass to keep her from suing me."

"What a complete prick."

I meant to only think it, but I said it out loud.

"What? Who?" Joe asked me.

"Never mind."

"Posner?"

He'd followed my line of sight and guessed who I was talking about.

"Yeah."

"He did sound a little insincere."

I sighed but didn't take my eyes from the conversation. Posner told Lance he and his crew would be taking a break for a couple of months, *to recover from their loss.* My mind added a sneer to his voice at this last statement. Lance walked away and Posner praised Jake for coming to the rescue. He specifically asked about me and my performance.

"She did great."

"No hesitation? You usually find hesitation in women." Posner looked directly at me, causing Jake to look my way, as well. I nodded to them both and threw them the most disingenuous smile I could muster.

"Not one bit of hesitation. She dropped eight men and didn't bat an eye." Jake gave me a return nod and a genuine smile.

He knew exactly how many men I'd taken out in Sudan. Why had he even asked me? Was it just common courtesy to let the killer tell you how many he's done, like asking someone about their number of sexual partners?

Posner continued their conversation. "You still sure she's an asset?"

"Yep."

"Fine. You can keep her. I've got a low-key job for you next weekend if you want it."

"What is it?"

"Cheap and easy security detail at the Civic Center and Arena. Some concert."

"That's kid's stuff, Mark."

"Thought you might like a nice break after Sudan."

"What's up with your security employees?"

"There's another convention that day and I was just informed that our guys didn't want to pull doubles. I can't blame them. They are just minimum wage rent-a-cops."

"So you pull in the higher-grossing guys to fill the slack?"

"Don't worry, you'll be getting minimum wage."

"Fine. How many to fill the slack?"

"A group of ten should cover it."

"Consider it covered."

Jake and Posner clicked their glasses together and then downed their drinks. Posner refused another glass when one of the girls approached them with her bottle of champagne, but handed her his glass. Then he left the rest of us alone with our champagne and the targets.

Jake walked over to Joe and me. "You two up for a minimum wage security detail for a concert?" he asked.

"Sure," Joe said.

"As long as we get paid," I said.

Jake's earlier remark still ate at me. At least I wasn't getting paid to shoot people this time. Maybe I wasn't cut out to be Penumbra. Then again, Penumbra made the world a better place. Maybe I wasn't cut out to work for Mesa.

"I'm going to go find Eric and see if he's up to it." Jake left me alone with Joe again.

"So, you and Jake an item?" Joe asked as soon as Jake was gone.

"What? No." I laughed.

"Are you going to be competition for any of these women?" He indicated the closest girl pouring champagne.

"Nope. Not *at all* my type."

"I'd hoped they wouldn't be. There's something very attractive about a woman who can handle a big gun."

I was caught off guard and was sure it showed.

I looked at the ground and then back at Joe. I'd never thought of Joe as a man I would be interested in. I pictured the two of us on a date. In a matter of seconds, my mind had us in my bed. He wasn't all that good-looking, but he had a rugged manliness about him. Stubble made his square jaw stand out and he wore the typically fit body that most of these men had. He'd definitely look good in swim trunks, or out of them. Plus, he knew how to handle his own sniper rifle. That was a definite pull for me.

I was sure Joe wouldn't be turned off by the fact that I'd been Penumbra in a past life and we could probably even start a *killer* business of our own. I doubted he had any of the right-versus-wrong hangups I had. None of these guys did.

I looked him directly in the eyes, seriously considering his offer. For some reason, the look he gave me made me blush.

He smiled a broad grin.

"It could be interesting," I mused. "But, I've already learned my lesson about dating coworkers."

"Let me know if you change your mind."

"I will."

I could still feel the heat on my face when Eric and Jake came back to us.

Jake wore a scowl, and Eric looked amused.

"You two ready to go?" Eric asked.

I didn't realize I had a grin on my face until Eric confused me with his question and I screwed up my face to ask, "Go where?"

"We always go out bar hopping after we get home from a gun battle," Jake said.

"Oh. I think I'll pass. I still have Africa all over me." I patted my pant leg and a plume of dust rose up.

"That's the point," Joe said. "The bus is ready?" he asked Eric.

"Yep. I even talked the girls into joining us." Eric wagged his eyebrows.

"Yo!" Eric yelled to get everyone's attention. "The bus leaves in two minutes. Everyone better be on board. You see those two over there, bro?" Eric pointed for Joe's benefit. "They're waiting for us."

The two girls sent flirty waves our direction.

Joe looked at me, as if to ask permission. I smiled and mimicked Eric's eyebrow wag.

I couldn't stop a giggle after he scurried away with Eric.

"What was that about?" Jake asked me, still scowling.

"Looks like Eric and Joe might get laid. You might want to go nail some of that down."

He rolled his eyes. "Shall we?" He made a flourish with his arm toward the bus.

"I told you, I'm not dressed for it."

"You *are* going. This is a ritual, and you will not mess with ritual." He took me by the elbow and gave a rough tug.

"Joe! Alex says she's not going," Jake yelled across the mob of men piling onto the bus.

"Hell no!"

I found myself swarmed by men, and being lifted onto the bus.

Someone yelled, "Our sniper bitch ain't sitting out of the hard part!"

I grinned and allowed them to pass me through the doors, dust and all.

THE HALF-NAKED WOMEN WERE JUST as affectionate to me as they were to the men on the bus. I was already tipsy from the champagne by the time we reached the first bar.

The lush bus seat was hard to leave, but I didn't linger. I wanted to avoid being carried off the same way they'd carried me on.

Once inside, I went straight for a table. Jake followed me and the rest of the men created a long line around the bar, waiting to be served.

Jake sat beside me, not saying anything as we watched the scene unfold around us.

Was this truly my new home? Were these the people I'd be spending my time with? When I took the job, I hadn't intended to stay long. Just kill some time until something happened to get me back to where I belong. That something hadn't happened yet, and it had been almost a year of waiting. A third of that time I'd spent with this company. I hadn't made friends with any of the men, except Jake and Joe, but I was getting comfortable.

I still ached to go back to White and Associates and be Penumbra on the side, but I couldn't imagine how that would come about.

Should I put it all aside and embrace this life? I looked over at Jake. He was watching me. I didn't have to worry about a huge secret any more. That opened up so many more opportunities for my love life. I could date him, or Joe, or anyone else. Maybe, expecting a man to give me the same chills White gave me was expecting too much.

I let my eyes wander to Joe. His lap was filled with the busty girl from the bus. What if I was her? I wouldn't sit on his lap in public and let him fondle me.

I looked back toward Jake, but he was gone.

Where did he go?

I caught myself straining my neck to see around the room. He was at the bar. A wave of relief settled over me when he came into sight.

Have I really become that attached to him?

My alarm at not knowing where Jake was confused me. I'd thought of Jake in the carnal sense, but never as a serious partner, at least not consciously. Yet, if I didn't think of him seriously why would I feel panic when I didn't know where he was? How could something like this sneak up on me?

I watched Jake walk back toward our table, a beer in one hand and a shot in the other.

"If you want anything else, there's a running tab at the bar." He handed me the shot. "Posner always lets the guys have a night out on the company after a job like the last one."

"Ones in which his people are killed?"

"Not just the ones where people are killed, but the jobs that include actual gunfire with the enemy. He understands the men need to blow off steam after something like that."

"I think I've had enough." The thought of drinking on Posner's dime was repulsive. I set the shot on the table.

"You have to drink it. We'll be toasting our lost friends and it'd be disrespectful not to join in on the toast."

The group of men started surrounding our table. In a matter of seconds, we all had our drinks in the air. Not a word was said and the silence made it feel more profound. Even if Posner had no respect for his men, they respected one another.

We only stayed long enough for the men who'd ordered something other than a shot to finish their drinks before we were off to the next establishment.

"Jake?" I asked once we'd taken our seats on the bus after the fifth bar.

"Yeah?"

"How many bars are we going to hit up?"

"As many as we can before they close."

"I won't be able to make it through." I was already slurring my words and could feel my stomach churning.

"You're with me. You'll be fine."

"Seriously, I can't. I can barely focus right now."

"Stop drinking the champagne on the bus and I'll take care of you at the next bar. Promise." He gave my hand a squeeze as he took my champagne glass away.

I'd been drinking a lot more since I'd taken up with these men, but the repeated shots of whiskey mixed with the champagne was more than I could handle.

I went through the motions of getting out of the bus and finding a table to occupy while the men made their orders. It seemed like an eternity before Jake came back with my shot. I needed that eternity to be able to focus on taking it from his hands.

"Last one. I promise," he said when I glared.

The men had congregated once again and we silently drank down our tribute.

As soon as the booze hit my stomach I could feel it trying to work its way back out. Jake was already by my side helping me up.

He stood at the door while I hung my head over the toilet in the women's restroom.

"That'll get rid of what you haven't digested yet. It should give you at least another hour before you're at your limit again."

"What the hell was in that shot?" I asked between my retching.

"Peppermint schnapps. I figured the peppermint would either settle your stomach, put you over the edge or bring about this reaction. You must really be drunk if you couldn't taste it."

I groaned and he laughed.

When my stomach settled somewhat, I came out of the stall and washed my face in cold water while Jake watched.

A couple of women walked in past him with disapproving expressions. I received the same looks when they saw me staring at my wet face in the mirror.

"Jake. I'm done. I can't lose control like this." I patted my face dry.

"That's the point, Alex. You need to rely on us to protect you and this is an easy test of that trust."

"I think I trusted you all well enough in frickin' Sudan. Holy shit. We had people shooting at us and you didn't see me hiding because I was afraid you guys didn't have what it takes."

"You didn't hide because it's against your nature. So, don't try to convince me you trust us because of that. It won't hurt you to get shit-faced with us." He was starting to slur as much as me. "And," he added, "we shouldn't discuss jobs inside a public women's toilet."

"Whatever. I am shit-faced. Consider me done. If we're all here to protect one another, as you say, then you should respect me when I say I'm done drinking."

"Whoa. You don't cave to peer pressure very well." He let the bathroom door shut after I walked under his arm. "Fine. Bottle of water at the next bar?"

"A bottle of water would have been perfect at *this* bar."

"I was hoping to get you as drunk as I did the first time we went out drinking."

"I think I'm past that point."

"Should we start a fight?"

"You're the only one I want to punch right now." I gave him a shove and he lost his balance. Thankfully, he stumbled into Eric and not the huge guy standing next to Eric. I didn't know who the big guy was, but I knew he wasn't part of our group.

"Watch it, man!"

Eric shoved Jake back my direction. Jake fell into me, I lost my footing and ended up on the floor with him on top of me.

Someone lifted Jake off me and gave me his hand.

"This is familiar," said Helix's voice through my fog.

"Helix?" I squinted and recognized him.

"Hey, babe. You okay?"

He moved his hand to the back of my head and felt around. It stung.

"I'm fine."

I pulled away from his prodding.

"Does this look fine?"

He held his hand in front of my face. It was covered in blood, a lot of blood.

"Shit. How did that happen?" I reached back and felt the hot blood on the back of my head.

"You hit your head, babe. Let's get you out of here, okay?"

Helix's voice was quiet and more gentle than I'd ever heard it. He put his arm around my waist and started to lead me away.

"Hey! Where you going with her?" I heard Jake demand from directly behind us.

"Your drunk ass knocked her into that table over there and she banged her head a good one."

I started to feel even more wobbly. If Helix hadn't had a good hold of my waist, I would have probably fallen to the ground.

"You want to come along to the hospital or do you want to stay here and party?"

"I'm coming," Jake said, all signs of a slur gone now.

"I'm fine." I tried to squirm away, but the dizziness got the best of me.

Jake took my hand and showed me the blood on it.

"I don't think you're fine. You need stitches and you might have a concussion. I told you, you needed to trust us."

The two men led me out of the bar and into the back of Helix's Cadillac.

"This is a brand new car. Helix, you better let me out before I get blood all over it."

"Jake. Get your ass in the back seat and keep her there," Helix ordered as he slid into the driver's seat.

He turned around in the seat and grabbed my arm while Jake pushed me further into the car by my legs.

"Leather seats, babe. They clean up good."

Chapter Twelve

"KEEP HER AWAKE, JAKE. I swear man, if she's seriously hurt I'm gonna kick your fucking ass. And, when I'm done, you'll have all her ex-partners on your ass, and worse."

"Her fucking partners?"

"Hey," I said weakly. "I don't have any partners any more. I quit working for them—" I tried to calculate the time that had passed, but couldn't. "Ages. I haven't worked with them in ages. It's been so long I can't even count that high. They piss me off, anyway."

"Girly," Helix said, his tone softening for me, "you just relax. I've got your back."

"Helix, shut the fuck up and just drive," Jake said.

"Don't rile me up, Jake."

"Helix. I'm fine." I sat up straighter, lifted my chin, and tried my best to not let my eyelids droop.

"We'll see about that soon enough." Then he growled, "Jake. Keep her awake."

"I'm awake," I opened my eyes. "I just have a headache."

"Sensitive to light?" Jake asked.

"No, just a throbbing head."

"Are you still dizzy?" Helix asked the next question.

"Yeah, but I think that's the alcohol."

They fired questions at me all the way to the hospital. I had to answer those same questions again while the doctor shined a light in my eyes, and stitched me up. I did get a few seconds to myself after Jake's ringing phone made me wince. The doctor gave Jake a reproving look when he took the call.

"You're going to be fine, Ms. Grey. Just keep the wound clean, and don't drink so much next time."

The doctor started giving Helix and Jake further instructions so I took the opportunity to curl up into a ball on the bed while I waited. He'd given me something for the pain, but it hadn't kicked in yet.

I FOUND MY WAY TO the bathroom with no trouble before I realized I was back at my room at Mesa. I hovered over the toilet for a few minutes then stood up and brushed my teeth.

"Everything okay in there?" Jake's voice came through the door.

"Go away. I'm fine."

"We need to know if you're getting sick." Helix's voice came through next.

I opened the bathroom door before I spit out my toothpaste. "What are you doing in my room, Helix?" I tried not to sputter out too much white toothpaste foam in my shock.

He smiled and wiped a couple of splatters off his shirt. "I'm protecting your virginity."

"I'm not a virgin!"

"Nice to know."

I sighed and went back to brushing my teeth. The men hovered at the door until I finished.

"I'm going back to bed," I announced.

"It's noon," Jake said.

"Noon?"

"Yeah."

"Do we have plans today?"

"No."

"Then I'm going back to bed."

"You sure you're fine?" Helix followed to the side of my bed.

"I'm hung over, but I'm fine."

"I'm talking about your stitches. Do you remember that?"

"Yes. I remember that. Dumbass Jake," I pointed at him, "knocked me over and I hit my head. You had a fit in your car. Oh, your car. Let me pay to have it cleaned. I'm so sorry, Helix." I got up off the bed and pulled out some cash I had in a jar on the dresser.

I pressed the money into his hands as he objected. "No, beautiful. It's all good. That's what friends are for."

"What's that? Bleeding all over your pretty leather seats? No. You take this and if you have to replace anything, let me know. Jake might have been the dumbass who knocked me over, but I'm the dumbass who got that drunk."

"Nah. It's all good. Jake already had it detailed. Plus, he told me about the job in Sudan. No one can blame the lot of you for needing to tie one on."

He took the cash and put it back in my jar.

"You shouldn't leave this much cash on your dresser, girl."

"I suppose not."

"You're in good hands. I'm going to get outta here. I had to call someone to open the gym. I'm a little afraid to show up this late."

"Thanks, Helix." I took his hands in mine again.

"That's not good enough."

He reached down and picked me up into a gentle hug. His gentleness never ceased to amaze me because of his size.

I couldn't help it. I kissed him on the cheek.

"I knew I'd get another one of those if I got you close enough."

He set me down tenderly. His smile dropped from his face and his brash speech lessened as he lowered his voice.

"If you ever need me, don't hesitate to call. For anything, you understand?"

I reached up and took his face in my hands. I had to stretch to the tips of my toes to get where I wanted to be. The kiss I gave him this time was on the lips. It was a gentle thank you and I was certain Helix would understand its meaning.

"Thanks again, Helix," I said when I went back to my natural height.

"That's my girl."

Helix drew me in for one more gentle hug before he left me alone with Jake.

"YOU SHOULD GO GET SOME sleep, Jake."

"Helix was the one who stayed up all night. I fell asleep on the couch. He didn't trust me to watch over you, I guess."

"I *am* going back to bed. I have a headache," I complained.

"I ordered some food. It should be here any time now, so you can't go back to bed. Besides, the doc told us not to let you sleep too much, anyway."

Jake handed me a couple of pills.

"Tylenol. He said you shouldn't need anything stronger."

He walked to the mini refrigerator and brought back a bottle of water.

"Thanks."

I sat on the couch and Jake joined me.

"Here, turn a little."

I did as he instructed and he started to rub my shoulders.

"I didn't mean to knock you over." His voice was so low I almost couldn't hear him.

"Not a big deal. I didn't even get a concussion," I said.

My door opened and Eric walked in. "I bet you aren't moving too fast today." He smirked.

"I'd like to not be moving at all, but Jake won't let me go back to bed."

"You whine too much."

This statement made me raise my eyebrows and stopped me from saying any more.

"Joe's bringing the food," Eric said as if he hadn't just been a jerk. Then he plopped down on the couch, picked up the remote, and turned on the TV, making sure to put the volume up louder than it needed to be.

I took the remote from him and turned the volume down. "I take it you didn't get laid last night?"

"I got laid," he said. "Just think you're milking this head injury crap."

"Okay, then. If you call wanting to go back to bed because I have a headache from the hangover as much as the bump on the head milking it—"

"No. I don't care if you want to sleep the day away, but why do you need an outside bodyguard?"

"You mean Helix?"

"Yeah, I mean Helix."

"I didn't ask him to stay. I was passed out."

"It's just funny that now you're here, we've had a run-in with Black. And now Helix."

"Helix was trying to be helpful, Eric," Jake said.

"The hell he was. He made it very clear he thinks she's too good for Mesa. If she's too good to work with us, then I say get the fuck out."

"And this is my fault?" My headache wasn't getting any better.

"Hell yeah, it's your fault. You've got all the men fooled. They can't see past your tits. I don't think you ever quit working for White and Associates."

"Why the hell would I be here if I were still working with White and Associates?"

Jake shot Eric a look that indicated he should shut up.

"You can't tell me she doesn't know, Jake."

"Know what?" I asked.

"Nothing," Jake said.

"What is it I'm supposed to know? I've been with you guys for a while now. If you think I'm hiding something, I have a right to know what it is."

Joe wheeled in a tray of food.

"Lunch," he said into the hot silence.

He took a step back, raised his hands, and shrugged. "What?"

"What is it I'm supposed to know that has Eric accusing me of still working with White and Associates, like I'm some kind of spy?" I asked.

"Have no idea. We going to eat?"

I moved to the tray and took a sandwich. Then I rolled the tray out the door. "Out." I pointed at the men standing in my room and drew a line from them to the tray standing outside the threshold.

Eric was the first to leave, then Joe. Jake hung back.

"Alex, it's nothing. Eric is just hung over."

"Forget it. I'll be out this afternoon." I put my hand on his chest and backed him out of the room while he tried to object. As soon as he was out I shut the door and locked it.

I sat at the table and ate my sandwich. Jake spent most of that time knocking on my door. When it finally became quiet, I packed up my things.

At least I don't have much.

I put two filled bags on the bed, stuffed my laptop under my arm, then picked up the bags again.

Eric met me right outside the door.

"You know if you leave it's just going to prove my point."

"What *is* that point, Eric?" I dropped my bags and was pleased to see I timed it just right for my laptop to land on top of them without hitting the ground.

"You don't give a shit about Mesa."

"All you had to do was ask and I would have told you. I *don't* give a shit about Mesa. It's just another company with another prick who owns it. I'm only here so I can work regularly. No other reason."

Jake came around the corner, followed by Joe.

"Alex," Jake started.

I held my finger up in an attempt to stop him.

"No. I will not find myself in the same situation twice. Actually, I have, but I'm leaving sooner rather than later." I turned back to Eric. "Eric. You better back off or I'm going to kick your ass. Just give me an excuse, actually."

Eric's top lip curled up and Jake hurried to reach us.

"Don't get involved, Jake," I warned.

Jake didn't slow his advance and Eric cocked back his arm before Jake could cross the distance.

I smiled and waited for it.

Eric's fist came for my face and I ducked just in time. He buried his hand into the wall up to his wrist.

I kneed him in the groin and watched as he doubled over, all his air escaping. The only things that kept him upright was one hand on his knee and the other stuck in the wall.

"I wasn't sure kicking you in the balls would have any effect. I have to admit, I'm surprised."

Eric growled at my comment.

Jake had covered the distance and Joe was right beside him.

"I'm playing with Eric, not you two. Either of you gets involved and I'll start taking this fight seriously." I felt my nostrils flare.

Jake and Joe took a couple steps backward.

Eric had caught his breath and was working to get his fist out of the wall.

"Hurry your ass up. I'm not done with you."

Eric freed his hand and took a stance. "Let's go, bitch," he said. He shook his hand as if to shake away the broken bones.

"We have jobs—" Jake didn't get to finish his sentence before I kicked Eric in the knee. He went down on top of my bags.

"Alex!"

I started pacing while Eric tried to stand.

"I should have done this to Red when I left. You're worse than he is, though. So, you'll definitely do."

I shouldn't be enjoying this so much.

I kicked Eric in the gut and he was back on the floor.

"Get up."

"Alex! Enough!"

"Stand his ass up so I can break his nose and then I'll quit."

"Someone get over here and help me up so I can break *her* nose!" Eric demanded.

"You heard the boy. Help him out." I pointed to him on the floor.

Neither of the guys went to stand him up so I walked back into my room and brought back a chair for him to steady himself on.

"Here. Use this. I promise I won't hit you until you're upright."

Eric growled again, but used the chair to steady himself.

"You think you can get a punch in?"

He dove for me and knocked me to the floor.

The pain, when I hit my head on the floor, made me see stars and I could feel the hot blood gush through the split stitches. I laughed.

"Finally. I could have killed you four times already."

I squirmed out from under him and pushed his face into the floor, hard. I heard bones crunching and he yowled.

"How's it feel to get your ass totally kicked by a girl, you dick," I said.

Joe and Jake watched as I picked up my bags and laptop.

I started to walk away and was met with Posner in the middle of the hallway.

"Pardon me," I said as I tried to step around him, but he wouldn't let me pass.

"That's what I like to see, Ms. Grey," he said.

"Good for you. Maybe you should get yourself some tickets to the fights, then. If you'll excuse me, I've got a road to get down."

I tried to pass again, but he snapped his fingers and, almost like magic, Joe and Jake stood on either side of him.

"You've got to be kidding me."

I dropped my bags again and this time my laptop didn't make such a smooth landing.

"I've had my reservations about you, but it's good to see you won't hold back."

"If I hadn't held back he'd be dead."

Jake and Joe both smiled, surprising me.

"As you can see," he continued as if I hadn't even spoken, "I'm down a man and could actually use the help. I'd be pleased to keep you on at Mesa."

"As you can see," I pointed to my bags, "you are down two men. Now, let me pass."

"If you insist. However, I'd appreciate it if you'd consider completing the jobs you've already been contracted for, and possibly keeping me in your Rolodex."

I relaxed somewhat, assuming this meant I wouldn't have to fight my way out.

"I could consider freelance."

"Good, Jake will get you set up. I'm sure he can still use the help with this upcoming concert security job."

Posner left me standing there, waiting for Jake and Joe to move so I could leave.

"You're still doing the concert job?" Jake asked.

"Is it still minimum wage?"

"Yep."

The smirk on his face told me he was impressed.

"You have my number. Call me with the time I need to show up for work this weekend." I stepped between him and Joe.

"Good to see big guns aren't all that you're good at," Joe said.

Chapter Thirteen

MY HEAD WOUND WAS BLEEDING steadily as I marched away from the facility. I waited until I got a significant distance down the road and around a couple of corners before I stopped to rest.

My stomach was protesting the sandwich I'd eaten and the sun seemed extra bright. I couldn't decide if it was my hangover causing these sensations or if I ended up with a concussion after the second blow to my head.

Whatever was going on, I didn't feel well enough to continue to walk so I sat on one of my bags beside the road and put my head in my hands.

Less than five minutes later, I heard a vehicle approaching.

I stood up and put a pack on each shoulder. I didn't want anyone to see me feeling sorry for myself on the side of the road.

Helix's Cadillac sped up to me.

"Hey. Hop in," he said after rolling down his window.

I pulled open the back door, noticed the back seat was still covered in blood, and tossed in my bags on top of the mess.

"Jake called and asked me to come out this way and make sure you were okay. He said you left on foot. You didn't get far."

I slid in the passenger door.

"Damn. You're bleeding again. Eric did this?"

He wasn't very gentle when he pushed me forward to take a look at the back of my head.

"Why would you assume Eric did it? What if I just fell and hit my head?"

"Jake told me you taught Eric a lesson and walked out. So, you're a free agent now?"

"I guess so."

"Good for you. If you won't go back to Black, freelance is the next best thing. Mesa is okay for the start-ups or the guys who don't care how they make their money, not fitting for you."

"I don't know. I didn't mind it. The guys seemed like good guys. All except Posner and Eric, anyway."

"So, tell me Eric looks worse than you do."

I laughed.

"Much worse. He won't be walking for a while. If I didn't break his kneecap, I know I over extended his knee. Plus, he broke his hand when he missed my face and punched the wall, and—" I laughed again, "I broke his nose."

"Eric's had it coming to him for years but everyone's been afraid to touch him."

"I don't understand why. He's pretty worthless at hand-to-hand. The only reason I'm bleeding is because he tackled me and my stitches broke when I hit my head."

"He's Posner's nephew."

Helix laughed deeply.

"All humor aside, you're going to need a place to stay. Somewhere away from Posner's radar. When he hears about this, you're probably going to have to dodge a few more punches."

"Posner was standing right there when it happened. He's the one who asked me if I'd work freelance when I refused to stay at Mesa."

"He actually let you leave the facility?"

I shrugged in answer to his question.

"He's very protective of family," Helix continued. "The last internal fight involving Eric landed the other guy in the hospital for a month. You can guess it wasn't Eric who put him there, either."

Helix and I rode along in silence for a few miles before his phone rang.

"Yo! Jake." Helix answered via the Bluetooth in his Caddy.

"You get her?"

"Yep."

"Hi, Jake," I said.

"Take me off speaker, man."

"Can't. I'm driving." Helix winked at me.

"Fine. Give me a call when you get to the hospital." He disconnected.

"I don't want to go back to the hospital."

"I've already got a doctor on the way to the gym to take care of ya. But, if he says hospital, you will go."

"Fine." I rested my head in my hands.

"Lean your head back, it'll be more comfortable," Helix said.

"No. I'm done getting blood all over your car."

"Don't you worry one little bit about that. I'll get it taken care of tomorrow."

"You told me Jake took care of it," I lifted my head to confront him.

"I know it. He will. Just not until tomorrow."

"The longer it sits, the harder it will be to get out."

"It's all good. Just relax. We'll be at the gym in about half an hour."

"So, is this you telling me to shut up?"

"On this subject, yes."

His deep rumbling laugh made me smile.

TRUE TO HIS WORD, WE pulled up behind the gym in about half an hour.

Helix hurried to the passenger side to help me out of the car.

"Helix, I'm fine." I refused the offered hand.

I couldn't stop him from opening the gym door for me and walked in without objection. He led me past the gawking patrons toward his office and had me lay down on his couch.

"The doc should be here soon."

When he left me alone, I sat up and wondered how I'd clean up the bloody mess off the leather couch. I searched around the office and found a small pile of towels in the corner. I imagined they had to clean up bloody messes from time to time, like when Jake and I'd broken each other's noses.

I wiped up the mess before it could dry and pressed the towel to the back of my head. The pain from pressing on the back of my head made me slightly lightheaded, so I put my head between my knees, being sure to keep the towel in place.

When Helix's office door opened again, I didn't look up.

"The doc's here, Alex." Helix said.

"Just have him stitch me up," I answered.

"How'd this happen, Helix?" Blue's voice held no hint of forgiveness.

I sat straight up and the change in blood flow made me swoon. I had no better word for it. My vision started to close in around me and weakness surrounded me. I fought against falling forward on my face, but only managed to deviate my fall a few inches to my left before I lost all motor control.

"Whoa," Blue's voice was tinny. I felt his hands on my shoulders, steadying me before I went all the way down. I fought to remain conscious.

When my eyes focused in on his face, I felt a wave of terror come over me.

"You gonna stay with me?"

I blinked several times, then nodded.

"Still lightheaded?" Blue dug around in his bag for his pen light.

"No. I think I just sat up too quickly."

"You've lost quite a bit of blood. You going to be able to relax for a couple days?"

"Probably."

"Make sure you do. I'm not in a position to give you orders any more, but I hope you'll take a doctor's advice."

I was subjected to the exact same exam I'd had the night before, but Blue checked my reflexes and asked me more personal questions. "How long ago were these stitches put in?" Blue asked.

"Last night."

"So, you got into a fight last night?"

"No. The fight was just a little while ago."

"How long ago?"

"I don't know, maybe an hour ago?"

Blue looked at Helix for confirmation and Helix nodded.

"So what happened last night?"

"We'd just got home from Sudan and were drinking to the memory of the seven guys Lance lost over there."

"What were you doing over in Sudan?"

"Helping Lance, and the guys he had left, get out of the country. What does this have to do with my head?"

"Just checking your long-term memory. If you can remember a couple days ago, it's a good sign."

Blue looked up at Helix. "I'm going to stitch her up now. Can you leave us alone for a bit?"

"No prob, doc."

Blue instructed me to lay on my stomach so he could get a clear shot at the back of my head.

"Can you make it quick?" I asked.

"We have to wait for the local to take effect."

He stuck me with a needle. It felt like he stuck it right in the middle of my wound and I winced. "Hold still. I'm almost done." He jabbed me again. "It's good to see you, Alex. We were all worried for a long time. Where have you been? I know you haven't been with Mesa all this time."

"Here and there," I said through clenched teeth.

"Do a lot of jobs as, you know? I haven't seen any mention of anything like that in the news."

"Nope. Put that life behind me. White won't be my handler any more," I cleared my throat to try and get rid of the lump. "I guess I'm retired."

"You okay, Alex? I mean, are you happy at Mesa?"

"I don't work for them any more, I'm a free agent again."

"Good. None of us really liked the jobs you were doing for Mesa, anyway. Can you feel this?" He poked something sharp into the gash.

"Yes! I feel that."

"Okay, I'll give it a little more time to numb up. So, why did Helix call me to stitch you up?"

"I have no idea. Maybe he wants me to kiss and make up with the company."

I could feel Blue pushing around on the back of my head.

"But why? Helix is his own man and he rarely does anything that doesn't bring him some kind of gain. I don't know how this would benefit him."

I didn't get it, either.

"Okay. All done." Blue said.

"What?" I thought we were still waiting for it to get numb.

"All done." He stood up from the couch and sat on the edge of Helix's desk.

I reached back to feel my stitches.

"Don't touch them. You can wash your hair later today. Just wait until you can feel the area. I don't want you to rip out your stitches again. That was a mess back there."

"Thanks." I stood up.

"Where are you going? Helix brought us together for a reason, we should try and figure it out."

"I thought I might ask Helix."

Blue grinned. "Good idea."

"Helix," I called out the door, then motioned him to us.

"Get her all fixed?" He asked Blue when he came into the office.

"Yep."

"You two talk?" Helix asked.

"That's the thing, Helix. We don't know what we are supposed to talk about. Maybe you can fill us in," I said.

"I just wanted to remind you that the company will always be here for you, if you need them." Helix told me.

I looked at Blue.

"It's true." He shrugged. "But, why would she need us, Helix?"

"She's working with Mesa. I'm sure she'll be needing you boys at some point to bail her ass out."

"That's true, too," Blue said.

"I don't believe you brought Blue here only to tell me he's here if I need him. What else did you expect him to tell me?" I asked.

"I thought he might fill you in on who you are working with."

Again, I looked at Blue.

"Mesa isn't a good place for anyone who has a history with us. Frankly, it's a dangerous place for you because of who you are. Posner has been on our list for years as well as the Admiral's short list, and he knows it. I can't give you details, but Posner is in deep with the Admiral. He's enemy number one. We were all surprised to know you were legitimately working for him and not in there at the request of the Admiral. Now, with that information, you can make a better-informed decision on whether or not you'd like to continue to work for the prick." He directed his attention back to Helix. "Why couldn't you tell her this, man?"

Blue was acting as if talking to me was a terrible chore.

"Thought it would be more compelling coming from you. Besides, it's not my place."

"You're right about that one, at least," Blue said. "Now she knows."

Then he walked up to me and gave my arm a good squeeze. "Helix is right about us being there for you if you *ever* need anything. The company isn't the same without you. I completely understand why you had to leave and don't fault you for it. I'll have a talk with White about that other thing. You shouldn't be blocked from your destiny because someone else decides to be stubborn."

"Thanks, Blue. For everything. But, please don't even tell White you saw me today. Like I said, I've left that all behind me. It's done, it's gone."

Saying it out loud wasn't easy, but saying it to Blue, someone who probably understood better than anyone else would, was an eye-opener. I caught myself swallowing extra hard to keep the emotion in check. I did *not* want to give up Penumbra. I'd always known that. It was the act of saying it out loud that nearly struck me to the floor.

"I KNOW A GUY WHO can find you an apartment, but it might take a couple days," Helix said after Blue left.

"Thanks, Helix. But, I'm going to be unreachable the rest of the week. I need a vacation."

I wasn't planning on a real vacation of any kind, but I wasn't in the mood to meet up with any more of my ex-partners, visit with Jake, or anyone else. I thought some time alone to reflect on this new information, no matter how incomplete it was, might be in order. I hadn't spent more than a couple hours alone since I'd started with Mesa. Jake had always been by my side. Now it was time to start thinking for myself again.

I'd do the concert security this weekend, but I didn't know if I'd do any more work for Mesa after talking with Blue. At least not until I'd taken the rest of the week to do more checking up on Mesa and Posner in particular. I wanted to know what the guys had against him and what my father had against him. My father didn't like very many people, but they never made a list unless they deserved it.

"Let me know if Jake doesn't take care of your Caddy," I said.

"Where are you going?" Helix asked as I opened the office door.

"I'll be around. I really appreciate everything you've done. I'm going to get my stuff out of the back seat of your car. Is it open?"

"It is now." Helix smiled as he pushed a button on his keychain. "Too bad that hard-headedness of yours didn't protect you last night and today. Kinda hoped Blue would have reined you in. I worry about you, Alex. Mesa is bad news. Actually, Posner is bad news. I got you out, now you need to run. Just wish Blue had taken a hand. I would have helped him tie you up if he'd been up for that."

"He knows why I had to leave and why I can't go back. If only you could explain to the Admiral what you witnessed today. Explain to him I can't go back, even if I wanted to. I only went to Mesa because *he* won't give me work."

"The next time I see your dad I'll be sure to let him know." Helix's eyes were sad as he looked at me.

I didn't realize Helix knew the Admiral was my father. I maybe should have been worried he knew that much about me, but I didn't care.

"I just wish I knew exactly what happened at White and Associates. Maybe I could help out more," he said.

"If I told you, I'd have to kill you."

Though the statement was used by people as a joke, Helix didn't laugh. He must have realized it was true in this case.

Chapter Fourteen

B*ACK TO HOTELS.*
I tossed my bags in the corner and eased myself onto the bed. My head throbbed and my stomach churned.

I stayed still on the bed for at least an hour before I gave up on sleep. My laptop was already next to me on the bed, so I opened it. I signed in using my Penumbra access. I wanted all the information I could get, but I couldn't get in. I tried to get into the government database at least ten times before I slammed the laptop closed in frustration.

I pulled out my phone and dialed my father's number.

"Hello?"

He already sounded smug.

"Why did you block me out of the database?"

"I thought you already knew. All past employees' access are revoked after they fail to renew their contracts."

"So, I'm totally cut off?"

"No. I'm sure you're welcome to utilize C.I.C. at White and Associates."

I hung up and threw the phone across the room.

The sobs came against my will. I knew crying would only make my headache worse and it was almost unbearable already.

WHEN I WOKE UP, I immediately looked at the time. It was four A.M. I could only hope I'd slept through several days. My head still ached, so I guessed I'd only killed the remainder of yesterday.

I retrieved the pieces of my phone from the floor. There was no saving it. I'd get a new one on my way to the airport. I consolidated my necessary items into one pack and lightened my load considerably. Then, took a shower.

The water felt like it was ripping my head open again, so I repositioned myself so it sprayed on the top of my head and ran down in a more gentle trickle. The blood that came out of my hair made the tub look like a murder scene. I pushed the dark water down the drain with my foot. The shower took me longer than I wanted it to because I couldn't just wash and go. I had to be careful.

After I toweled off I called a cab from the hotel phone.

I was at the airport within the hour. I booked the next departing flight. I didn't even listen to the destination. It was time to get out of here.

I had a couple hours to kill, so I went to the airport restaurant and had breakfast. My stomach still didn't want any intrusion, but I forced the food down and managed to keep it there.

Finally, the flight came in and I boarded. Two hours later I found myself at a different airport with nowhere to go.

I booked a room from my laptop and had a cab take me to the closest big box store so I could replace my phone. I didn't plan on calling anyone yet, but I wanted to get the chore out of the way.

ONCE INSIDE MY NEW ROOM, I tried again to get into the government database. I knew being in a different city wouldn't make any difference, but I had to try. I was right and didn't gain access. I considered going out to see the sights, but the bright sun deterred me from going out at all. Instead, I laid back on the bed and tried to watch television.

Eventually, I gave in and researched like normal people had to. I bought a background check for Posner and looked up his name in a worldwide newspaper article search.

I didn't get much. He'd been honorably discharged from service a couple years before White and Associates became a company, and started Mesa immediately.

Mesa had some dedicated articles to their credit. None of them were flattering. The articles accused Mesa of supplying guns and running drugs on a regular basis.

This made me wonder if the company might have known Danny was really transporting drugs, but only feigned innocence because of some outside reason.

My mind went to Jake. Did he know about this activity? Were these accusations true? The way Blue and Helix talked about Posner, I was inclined to believe Posner knew if Jake didn't.

How could Jake not know? *I* didn't know. But, I wasn't in the position to know. Jake was.

My desire to do the right thing was muted by the way I'd been treated because of doing just that.

My partners had disowned me because I'd taken on a higher role to make the world a better place. My mind had always fought with the idea of Penumbra as a mixture of good and evil because of the requirements of the job. But, after I'd lost her, I realized Penumbra was a necessary part of the world. She made it safer for the good people.

I had to remind myself that Red was the only one who was openly against my outside persona. Yet, they backed him. They had more history, I guess. The part that hurt me the most now was not my partners being a part of my past, or even the brief moment I got to love White, but my father pushing me out. He was my father. He made me, and now he wouldn't back me.

Quit feeling sorry for yourself.

He'd back me if I were willing to give up Red. I was certain, if I admitted Red knew I was Penumbra, Red would go missing and I'd have a brand new handler in a matter of minutes. In fact, I was fairly certain, my father already had someone lined up to be my handler. I suspected he'd put Colin in that position and White and Associates would cease to exist in their current form.

They'd become another Mesa. No more government contracts.

I could never do that to my partners.

I only had a couple choices. I could take my chances at Mesa or I could go on permanent vacation, picking up jobs where I could.

I DIALED JAKE.

"Yes?"

Hearing his voice was soothing, even though I was unsure of his good guy, bad guy status.

"Jake. It's Alex. I broke my phone, so this is my new number."

"Where are you?"

"In a hotel room."

"I've checked all the hotels. What name are you using?"

"Never mind that. I just wanted to touch base before this weekend."

"Let's get together for dinner," he said.

"Can't. I'm out of the city. I'm just calling to find out what time I should meet you this Saturday. I'll be sure to be back in town by then." I tried to keep my voice away from the friend zone and only use businesslike tones.

"Helix said he was going to set you up in an apartment."

"I'm not going to let Helix find me an apartment. It's best if no one knows where I am right now."

"I talked with Posner. He told me the reason he let you leave was because it was time for someone to put Eric in his place. He's allowing it because he figures you and Eric are more evenly matched than any of the men in the company. You don't need to worry about that."

"I'm not worried about that." I shook my head, even though I knew he couldn't see me. "Posner's an ass. Eric and I aren't evenly matched. He's so far below me, it's pathetic. I should probably be ashamed of kicking his ass if we want to look at it that way."

Jake laughed. "I'd still like to get together before the job this weekend."

"Nope. I'm out of town and don't plan on coming back until Saturday."

"Where? I'll join you."

"Give it up, Jake. I'm not meeting with you. I have some things I need to do."

"You really shouldn't take on any side jobs. Posner doesn't like that."

I was getting frustrated. "I don't work for Mesa any more. Remember? Maybe *you* should have your head checked instead of me. Posner doesn't own me. He never did. You should probably go freelance yourself."

"I like my job. Hell, if you come back and kick Eric's ass a few more times, I just might get back my second in command title."

"That reminds me," I said. "Is Eric still going to work the concert with you? It's probably best if I stay away from him for a while."

"He won't heal up before then."

I could hear the glee dripping from his words.

"Why didn't you ever tell me you didn't like Eric? Hell, why didn't you ever tell me he was Posner's nephew?"

"This is not a democracy, Alex. We have a monarch named Posner, and any opposition to the throne is treason. As for Eric being Posner's nephew, it never cropped up."

"Makes me wonder what else never cropped up."

I didn't want to get into all the sordid details right now, but I couldn't help but make the jab, anyway.

"Plenty, I can assure you. Sometimes it's best to be on the outside."

"And we make it back to the freelance word."

"Freelance isn't for me. I'm either going to own Mesa someday or I'm going to start my own business that'll compete with Posner. I'm still holding out for Mesa ownership at the moment. The second Posner's ready to sell, I've got my offer ready for him. I'd be willing to take on a partner. It's something you should consider."

That *was* something I could consider.

"I'll see you Saturday night, Jake." I hung up.

I SPENT THE REST OF the day in whatever city I'd managed to fly to, but hopped on a plane back home the next morning.

The remainder of my week was spent doing hard research on Mesa and Posner while periodically trying to gain access to the government database.

Chapter Fifteen

SATURDAY NIGHT CAME AROUND AND I was ready to get out of my hotel room. I arrived at the Civic Center half an hour before Jake told me to be there.

There were lines of people waiting to get in. The back entrance, where I was supposed to meet Jake, was surrounded by screaming fans.

Jake and Joe stood at the entrance of a roped off area.

"You're early," Jake greeted me.

"I got back into town a little early." It wasn't a lie.

"Nice to see you, Alex," Joe said, then walked off to attend the rope line.

"Since you're here, I'll tell you exactly what's expected of us. Ms. Moran has her own personal detail. We are just the backup provided by the facility."

"Angel Moran?" I felt a grin cover my face. "Will we get to meet her?"

I'd gone to one of her concerts with Gabriella about a year ago. It would be fun to actually meet her. I fought the urge to immediately call Gabriella to tell her about my luck.

"Yes. She'll be here in about fifteen minutes." Jake grinned at me. "Now, pay attention."

He told me all we had to do was make sure no one got in the building from the doors we were guarding.

"We won't get to see the show?"

"If you want, we can trade places with a couple of the guys after the band gets here. I just thought you'd enjoy this position better. This is where it'll go down if it does."

"Where are the rest of the guys?" I asked as we stood near the door.

"They are inside at their positions. Here."

He handed me a radio that I clipped to the top of my pants.

"How's your head?"

Jake leaned back in an attempt to see my gash.

"Fine."

I turned to face him directly. I didn't want him to start picking through my hair like a monkey.

"So, you like Angel Moran?"

"Love her!" My grin came back. "Just wish I was here for pleasure instead of work, now that I know it's her."

"When she pulls up, her personal guard will probably walk her inside. All we really need to do is hang out here and make sure no one gets past us."

Jake stood to one side of the door and motioned for me to stand at the other side.

A limo pulled up shortly after we took our places.

I watched as the driver got out and came around to the passenger side door, opened it and offered his hand.

I was slightly surprised when she stepped out. She wasn't all dolled up yet and looked very human. She was still gorgeous, but I might not have recognized her without her signature glittery makeup and sparkly outfits.

I must have looked like an idiot. I could feel my grin, but couldn't force it down until I saw who pushed his way out after Angel.

"Josh!" Angel's tone was offended as Brown pushed past her toward me.

My stupid grin was gone and I stood stoic and unmoved, like the Queen's Guard.

"What the hell are you doing here, Alex?" He stomped toward me.

I didn't answer him.

"Back off, Brown." Jake stepped between us.

"Hey, Jake."

The two shook hands as if Brown hadn't just charged me.

"Good to see you, Josh. Now, let us do our job?"

"Josh?" Angel questioned him from behind. "Who is she?"

Brown looked at Angel and back at me.

"Alex, this is Angel." He stepped out of the way. "Angel, this is Ms. Grey."

I held out my hand.

"Such a pleasure," I said. "I'm excited to see the show."

She didn't take my hand and directed all of her attention at Brown.

"*Ms. Grey? For real?* "

He smiled and nodded at my still outstretched hand.

"Josh talks about you all the time. The pleasure is all mine." She took my hand and gave it a tight squeeze.

"Come on. Join us in the V.I.P. room. I know you and Josh have a lot of catching up to do." She tried to pull me into the building after her.

"I can't. I'm working."

"What? My security?" She laughed. "You're funny."

"Yes. Security."

She looked shocked.

What the hell did Brown tell her about me.

I gave him a dirty look and he smiled back at me in that familiar devious way he had.

The remaining people from inside the limo had backed up behind us and I was starting to feel decidedly naked.

"Well, maybe your boss will let you chat with Josh through the door then?"

She looked Jake up and down, raising one of her eyebrows, then winked at me.

"Maybe," I said.

She finally let my hand drop and turned to walk inside. "You coming, Josh?"

"Nah," he said. "You go do your thing. I'm going to hang here."

"Have fun," she said.

I'd resumed my stance beside the door and Jake mirrored me on the other side.

Brown took up his own stance right next to me, looking very much the part of security.

After Angel Moran's entourage had filed into the building Brown grabbed me around the waist, lifted me and twirled around.

"Put me down!" I yelled.

He'd caught me off guard and I almost reacted badly, but after one spin I was smiling again.

"I missed you," I said.

He set me down and pointed toward Jake.

"What the hell are you doing working for these assholes? No offense, Jake."

Brown briefly glanced Jake's direction when he said this.

Jake had moved from his post and was closing the distance hesitantly. If I had objected too much to Brown's rough play, I'm sure Jake would have stepped in. He gave me a questioning look and I nodded back to make sure he knew everything was okay.

"Seriously, Alex. Why the hell are you doing security work for *Mesa?*"

"It's a job."

"We've got plenty of work for you. Come home."

"Home?" I laughed and shook my head.

"Yes, Alex. Home." Brown snubbed my dismissal.

I regained my position near the door. "This conversation is not going to happen here."

"The hell it ain't. This is the first time I've seen you since you left. I don't give a shit who's around, I don't care what's said. You've been M.I.A. for *months*. Don't you think we deserved some kind of explanation? Cuz, I think we did. You can't drop a bombshell, like you did, without some explanation."

"I didn't drop anything. Not a damn thing. I left because—"

"Okay. It wasn't you, it was Red. So what. It is what it is and I want to know more."

"Tough shit."

"I deserve it, Blue deserves it, Green deserves it, but most of all, Black deserves it. White won't open his mouth, but you better."

"I told you. I'm not having this conversation here."

"And I told you I don't care what you want. Not any more. You left us all out in the cold and it pisses me off. If we don't talk now, when? When? When I stumble across you at some other worthless Mesa job?"

Jake had moved to my side.

"Brown, even though I'd love to know what happened at White and Associates, she *is* working and I can't allow you to badger my employee."

"Shut up, Jake!" Brown and I said in unison.

"I had to leave. Red was acting like— I don't know what the hell he was thinking. He should have come to me or White first instead of having a company meeting. Have you given any of this any real thought? I suspect you haven't. Imagine *the powers that be* knew what Red knows. What do you think would happen? I left to keep *him* safe."

I watched the realization hit him.

"Red is a jackass, but he's not a threat."

"You go tell him you saw me and talked me into coming back. See how he reacts, then come find me at one of my worthless jobs. If you can tell me he's going to back down from the whole *Ms. Grey's a traitor* attitude, then maybe you and I will have something to talk about." I was shaking and on the verge of bawling. I unclenched my fists and took a few deep breaths.

"You don't know how much I want to come back and pretend that this never happened," I continued. "But Red isn't the only one who feels betrayed. He had Green following me around, spying on me. Green was a willing participant. Trust me, Josh. You are all better off without me and I'm better off being outside a company full of men who will never give me their full trust and partners who won't return the loyalty they expect from me."

"I still miss you," Brown said after a long pause.

"You have no idea how much I miss you." I hastily wiped a tear from my eye. "Now go have some fun with your lady."

"I'm sorry, Alex. You're right. I'd never thought about it from that direction. I'm so sorry."

"Yeah. Me too."

Brown set his jaw and walked into the building.

"Alex? You okay?" Jake asked.

I smiled. "I'm fine, Jake. Just tying up loose ends really sucks, you know?"

"What the hell happened over there?"

"I did some secret side jobs. Red found out and thought it was his place to let all my partners know."

"They didn't want you working outside the company. Posner doesn't like that, either."

He nodded his head as if he truly understood now. Something about his tone made me want him to know he still had no idea.

"White set up the jobs and encouraged me to take them. Red called me out on it and White didn't back me." I shrugged. "Those men have been partners since before White and Associates. I don't know why I expected White to fight for me. I'm just— an add on."

Jake didn't say another word. I held my chin a little higher reminding myself I'd done nothing wrong. Nothing. And, nothing I did would make me one of the guys. I was done trying to fit in.

A few seconds later, Brown stepped out the door with his phone to his ear.

"I'm on my way," he said into the receiver. "Alex. I've got to go. Something came up. You might want to call White.

But, I want you to know, you can call me *anytime*, for any-thing at all. Even if it's just someone to fight with. I'll never forget our sparring sessions." He waggled his eyebrows as he elbowed me in the arm.

I smiled and gave him a little push back.

"Seriously now," he put his phone in his back pocket and took me by the shoulders. "I don't want to lose you. Even if we can't work in the same company, for now, I will always be here for you." He kissed my forehead. It was tender and quick. Then, he pulled me into an embrace.

I fought hard to keep my emotions in check. When he pulled away, his gaze was intense.

"Always," he said. He walked briskly away and called back just before he was out of earshot. "Oh, and you really should call White."

Chapter Sixteen

JAKE LEFT ME ALONE WITH my thoughts until the concert started. I stood there wondering why Brown told me to call White. Was there trouble, or was he just trying to get me to call White? I had White's phone in my back pocket. I took it out to make sure it was on. If he needed me, he could call.

The music started. My initial excitement about seeing Angel in concert again had faded and hadn't found its way back to me.

"Did you want to switch out with a couple guys inside so you can see the show?"

"No. Thanks," I said.

Conversation ceased again. Nobody tried to cross the rope line and the crowd thinned. After what seemed like an eternity, the show was finally over.

I could hear the fans clamoring for more and heard the encore. When there was no sound but cheering fans, our radios crackled with an unfamiliar voice.

"Miss Moran is leaving now."

Being so close to Jake with my radio caused some feedback, so I shut mine off.

Jake spoke into the radio, but I didn't hear what he said.

The crowd was almost nonexistent by this time, but I readied myself when the limo pulled up to the curb.

The doors opened and her entourage filed out and started filling the limo. Angel was almost the last person out. She was followed by two of her personal guard.

She stopped beside me and took my hand in hers.

"I just want to say how much of a treat it was to meet you, Ms. Grey. Josh adores you and you should try to keep in better touch with him."

I didn't know what to say in return, so I nodded and smiled.

Though I'd never fit into their clique, I did have a special relationship with each of the men. Brown had become the brother I never had and treated me like a sister. Saying goodbye wasn't easy.

Angel Moran's grip remained strong and she held my gaze like a pro. I felt the tears trying to well up. I'd spent the night keeping my emotions in check. I couldn't let go, yet.

"Miss Moran." Thankfully, one of her guards interrupted us. "We need to get you into the car now."

She nodded, gave my hand a squeeze and moved toward the limo.

As soon as the limo drove off Jake asked, "You wanna get outta here? I can have Joe wrap things up here."

"Sure."

He called Joe on the radio and left me alone at the door while he retrieved his car.

When he pulled up, I slid into the passenger seat of his Charger.

"What do you want to do?"

"You can just drop me off at my hotel. I should get some sleep."

"Come on, Alex. I haven't seen you for an entire week. I want to know what you've been up to. You can't shut me out the way you did the colors."

That was a slap in the face.

"Pull over, Jake."

"What?"

"Pull over." My hand was on the door handle and shaking.

"I'm sorry, Alex. I didn't mean—"

"Just let me out."

His voice deflated. "I'll take you to your hotel. Which one is it?" he asked.

"I'll find my own way, thanks. Now pull the damn car over." My voice shook. "I don't want you to know where I'm staying. Just PULL OVER."

My anger at Jake's words diminished with his apology, but the energy hadn't dispersed. It had morphed into despair. I didn't think I could hold onto my emotions much longer. Where the hell was Penumbra's calm when I needed it?

"Alex. I just wanted to catch up. I'm sorry. Please, just tell me which hotel. I won't say another word."

I shook my head and muttered the hotel under my breath, then spent the ride watching out the side window.

He was true to his word until we pulled into the hotel parking lot. He asked if he could come up as I stepped out of the car.

"Suit yourself."

I got out and walked into the hotel without glancing back. He better keep up. I wouldn't wait and I wouldn't go looking for him if he couldn't find my room.

He managed and remained quiet as we rode the elevator up to my room.

His presence was reassuring. If he hadn't been at my side I probably would have already broken down. Even though it was his fault I'd gotten all worked up in the first place, I was thankful he'd come with me.

He followed me into the room and I went directly to my bathroom. I might have been glad he was there, but I wasn't ready to tell him that.

I killed time by taking a hot shower. Hot water has a tendency to relax me. I could hear the television and assumed he'd made himself comfortable.

I dreaded leaving the bathroom, so I dried and dressed slowly.

Please, don't talk.

I opened the bathroom door with that coursing through my mind.

Jake was leaning back on my bed, flipping through the channels on my television.

I climbed up onto the bed next to him. He only flipped channels a couple more times before he decided on a movie.

I WOKE UP TO A quiet and dark room. I tried to remember how the movie ended, but must have fallen asleep almost immediately because I couldn't remember more than ten minutes of the show.

I turned my head to look at the clock, but it wasn't there. I squinted and realized I could see the faint red glow of the clock behind Jake's form beside me.

"Hi," he said.

My stomach churned. "Hi. What are you still doing here?"

"You were having bad dreams. I thought I'd stay until you settled down or woke up."

"I'm fine, Jake."

Nervousness ate at me and I could feel myself shaking. I'd fallen asleep next to Jake before, but had never been confronted with him in a dark room.

I felt him moving on the bed, then felt his hand move my hair away from my face. My breath became shallow and my libido kicked into overdrive.

He must have realized this because he leaned in closer and kissed me gently. I let him kiss me once, then I kissed him back. The kisses became more and more intense as we lay there until we were both clawing to get our shirts off.

The heat of his body against mine was adding to my passion until he reached behind me to unhook my bra. A flashback of White doing the same came crashing in on me. I tried to push those thoughts away, but White's phone vibrated in my back pocket. Brown's voice entered into the equation. "You might want to call White." I was instantly sobered from my sex-drunk state.

I pushed away.

"Jake. I can't. I'm sorry."

I rolled to the edge of the bed and leaned over to search for our shirts in the dark, trying to ignore the vibrating in my back pocket.

"What's wrong?"

He slid up behind me and caressed my shoulders.

I still ached to be touched. Just not by him. Not with White in my back pocket.

"I don't think I'm ready, yet."

The phone vibrated again.

"I told you to ditch that damn phone."

I handed him his shirt, then pulled my own over my head.

"I'm sorry," I repeated.

"I really hate White," he said. "You going to answer it?"

"No. But, it killed the mood," I said.

I took the phone from my back pocket and put it into the top drawer of the nightstand.

"Just shut it off."

He reached for me again and I pulled away.

"You better get home. I'll call you in a couple days."

Jake followed me to the door.

"You going to be okay?"

"Yes, Jake. I'm fine. You don't need to treat me like a child," I said.

He nodded and his eyes flitted to the nightstand as the phone vibrated again.

"You should just talk to him. Get it over with and then maybe you can throw that damn phone away," he said.

I had every intention of answering the phone, but that was my business, not his. I was worried something was wrong. Brown's words kept leaking into my thoughts.

"I might. I'll talk to you soon. Promise," I said.

Jake stood outside my door still holding his shirt in his hands. I shut the door and watched through the peephole. He threw his shirt on and stared at the door for a few seconds. Finally, he stalked off.

I went to my nightstand, pulled out the phone, and dialed White.

"ALEX?" HE ANSWERED.

His voice was tired and drawn.

"Is everything okay?" I asked.

"I've got some bad news. Will—"

He took in a long shaky breath.

"I got a call a few hours ago. Will's plane went down. He's gone."

My heart broke and I lost all ability to speak for a moment.

Will was gone? White's little brother. The man I seriously considered over White when White was still available to me. The tears streamed down my face.

"You aren't alone, are you?" I asked.

"I kicked the guys out a while ago," he said.

"I'll be there as soon as I can." I hung up and packed my stuff.

The cab pulled up outside of White and Associates fifteen minutes later.

The night guard greeted me as I walked in. "Ms. Grey. Good to see you."

"Good to see you, Phil. I'm here to see White." I headed toward the elevator.

"I was told to give you your keys when you came back."

He'd rushed to catch up with me and held out the keys to my apartment.

I almost refused, but took them instead.

"White's expecting you at his apartment."

"Thanks, Phil," I said.

I got into the elevator and pushed the button for the eighth floor, White's apartment.

As the elevator rose, so did my anxiety. If I could get past the seventh floor, where the office was, I could see White without having to talk to any of my partners.

My luck didn't hold and the elevator slowed, then stopped on the seventh floor. I pushed buttons repeatedly, but the doors still opened.

Red and Black hesitated before getting into the car.

"Grey," Red greeted me. "I take it you heard?"

I ignored him. I was seething inside. His expression and tone were contrite, but I couldn't find any civil words in my vocabulary.

"If you're going to see White, we'll go up to my apartment," Black said.

I looked him in the eyes. They were full of sorrow. I'd expected that, but I'd also expected a bit of condemnation. There was none.

I nodded and got off on the eighth floor alone.

I knocked lightly on White's door.

He looked drained. "Thanks for coming. I know how you connected with Will." He eyeballed my two duffle bags.

"Sorry. I've been living out of these bags and just take them most everywhere I go," I lied. I wasn't sure why I had brought everything. It seemed like the thing to do.

He nodded and walked into his kitchen.

I followed and took a seat right next to him. I was sick with tension. "What can I do?"

His shrug was barely noticeable and he shook his head miserably.

We sat in the same positions for at least an hour before he put his head onto the counter.

"He was my little brother."

I stood from my chair and went to his side. He lifted his head from the counter and we clutched each other as we cried.

I never expected this much misery from him, ever. Though I was suffering from my own feelings of loss and despair, I cried for White more than I did for Will. The realization of this made me feel horrible. My heart ached at the loss of Will, but it shattered inside my chest at White's anguish.

We stayed like this for more than an hour. Eventually, White sat back.

"I'm so sorry, Alex. I never meant to—"

His eyes were sunk into his face, making me tear up again.

I wiped my tears away.

"What happened?" I asked.

"They didn't give me any details. Just said he'd gone missing about a month ago and they'd been trying to recover the aircraft and his body. They had no luck locating his body."

"A month and they're just telling you this now?"

"This kind of news isn't always fast in coming. They don't want to hand out false reports, so they keep it quiet until they're sure. He was deployed, so no news isn't uncommon."

I stood there awkwardly for a moment. I didn't know what to do next. I had no words of comfort. Nothing I said could help, so I followed my instincts and reached over and smoothed out his hair.

"I imagine you have somewhere to be," he said.

"No. Unless you'd like to be alone."

"No. If you can stay, I'd like that."

"Can I get you anything to drink?" I asked. I moved around the bar into the kitchen.

"No. Help yourself, though."

He moved to the couch and I followed.

"We're not going to hold a funeral. Well, I'm not sure what Mom and Dad are going to do. I'm not attending," he said.

"It might be better if you do."

"I'm glad you came. The guys are great, but I needed *you*." He changed the subject smoothly.

"Of course I came, White." I wanted to tell him he was still at the center of all my thoughts but it wouldn't come out. I was still too hurt by everything else. All I knew was, I'd be here whenever he needed me.

He'd started to look healthier since we'd moved to the couch. Color had returned to his face. At least that's what I thought until I realized the sun was coming up, giving his face the color.

"Alex." He took my hand in both of his.

My phone rang.

He dropped my hand. "Jake?" he asked with venom.

I pulled out my phone. I was sure it was Jake. He was the only one who called me. I nodded as I rose from the couch. "Hello?" I answered.

"Everything okay, Alex? Did you talk to him?"

"Something came up, Jake. I'll call you when I get time. Okay?"

"What's wrong?"

"I'll call you later. Promise."

"You're with White, aren't you?" he asked.

"Yes. I have to go. I'll be in touch later today."

"Okay."

I'd expected more of an argument. I was relieved he didn't fulfill my expectations. "Thanks," I said.

I hung up and returned to White's side on the couch.

After a couple minutes of silence White asked, "Are you and he an item?"

"No. He's just a friend, for now."

"For now?"

"Let's not do this. Okay? Now isn't the time. Will—" I said.

"No. Don't use the loss of Will to get out of this talk. I've been trying to have this talk with you for months. You're just as important to me as Will is and I have to know. If there is no chance we can work things out, I have to know."

"I don't know. I can't get past you still working with Red."

"You're telling me I have to choose?"

"He destroyed my *life*, White. My entire life. I don't have Ms. Grey any more. I don't have Penumbra any more. My father has cut me off completely. I don't even have *you*." My voice warbled.

"You'll always have me."

"You stood by and let him destroy my life, White. How can you say I have you?"

"I didn't just stand by and watch."

"Yes, you did. We were in contact for a month after all hell broke loose. You weren't able to convince him I wasn't a traitor to the company in that time. I *wanted* to come back. I still want to come back. But you told me to give him more time. You kept telling me to give him more time. I was done waiting for you to make up your mind." I took a breath. "I'm not the one who was forcing you to choose. He did that, and you chose him."

"I didn't choose anyone. There was no choice for me."

"There wasn't?" I shook my head and stood from the couch. I walked over to White and kissed him tenderly on the forehead. "White. I love you. I will always love you."

I walked to the door, picked up my bags and walked out. White was talking as I left, but I didn't hear anything he said.

I rode the elevator up to my apartment. Once inside, I cried.

The crying didn't last as long as I thought it would and when I wiped the tears away for the last time, I was determined. I cleaned out my bags and took a shower. When I was cleaned up and dressed I went to the kitchen and made some coffee. I didn't care if it was stale.

I called Black's apartment and invited him up.

Chapter Seventeen

B LACK WAS IN MY APARTMENT before the coffee was done brewing.

"It might be stale," I said while pouring his cup.

"That's fine. You back?"

"Not back with the company, no. But, I think I might hang out in my apartment for a while. As I understand it, I'm still a partner on the books."

He nodded and donned a sinister grin. "Took you long enough. Have any jobs lined up?" he asked.

"You mean Penumbra?"

"Anything."

"No. Dad cut me off from Penumbra because White won't be my handler and I won't rat out Red. I'm no longer on Mesa's steady payroll. I'm freelance. You have anything?"

"Nope."

"Pretty sure Jake'll keep me busy enough."

"About Mesa. Be careful," Black said.

"I will."

We sat in silence long enough to finish off the pot of coffee. It wasn't all that good.

"You going to Will's service?" he asked.

"I don't know. Do you know when and where?"

"Not yet."

He asked if I wanted to join him at the gym, but I declined. I had no plans for the day, but I wasn't ready to go back to business as usual, especially since it wasn't business as usual.

He left me alone in my apartment with the statement, "Glad you're home."

Black wasn't gone more than ten minutes when I received a knock at my door. I opened it up to find Brown and Blue outside.

"May we come in?" Blue asked as Brown pushed his way past me.

I moved aside so Blue could enter without having to squeeze past me.

"Black told us you were back," Brown started.

He was already in my kitchen pouring himself a cup of coffee from my freshly-brewed pot.

"I'm not back. I'm just going to stay in my apartment for a while instead of in a hotel room."

"You aren't going to start working again?" Blue asked.

"This is terrible," Brown complained about the coffee.

"It's old coffee, but it's all I had."

Someone else was knocking at my door.

I found Green outside, offering a fragrant bag of fresh-ground coffee.

"Black said I should come bearing gifts. He said you could use some coffee."

"Come in," I said.

Green was a touchy subject for me, still. He had been the one who had, ultimately, been the demise of Penumbra. If he hadn't done Red's bidding, I doubt anyone would have found me out. The only reason I wasn't entirely fed up with him was because he was proud of who I used to be, unlike Red.

"Thank the heavens!"

Brown met Green half way, took the coffee from him and went back to the kitchen to start a fresh pot.

The four of us sat at the kitchen bar and drank our coffee in silence.

Finally, Green said, "The Malones are having a service tomorrow evening. It'll be quick and quiet. Only family. We won't be invited."

"White said he won't go to any service," I said.

"It's understandable," Blue said. "This is a terrible loss for him and he's not ready to let go, yet. The Malones should have waited a little while." He shook his head.

I expected Brown to have something to say. I looked at him and saw tears in his eyes. He was probably the closest to

Will, other than White. It was him who'd tried to set me up with Will.

Will wasn't just White's little brother to Brown, he was his friend. His fellow pilot.

I sat, sipping my coffee, as the men did the same. It was quiet and, strangely, comfortable. It almost felt as if I'd never left.

My phone rang, breaking the comfortable silence.

Damn, Jake.

"Hello?" I answered.

"Did you get things worked out?"

I walked away from the men so I could have some privacy.

"Alex? Are you still there?" Jake asked.

I shut my bedroom door.

"Yes. I just wanted to get somewhere more private."

"Where are you?"

"In my apartment."

"What apartment?" he asked.

"At White and Associates."

"So, you *did* work everything out."

"I didn't go back to the company, but I needed a place to stay. White's brother was killed and I thought I should be here for my partners."

"Did you know him?"

"Yes, Jake. I knew him. Even if I didn't I wouldn't ignore my partners in a time like this."

"Sorry. I understand. How'd it happen?"

"Not sure. I guess his plane went down and they never recovered the body."

The line was quiet for a few seconds.

"So sorry to hear that. We're going to have that refinery job coming up. You still game?"

"Of course. When?"

"We leave tomorrow. Eric will be going. He'll have a brace on his knee, but he's going."

"Tomorrow?" I didn't know if I should leave so soon. I worried about White and was starting to enjoy the comfortable feeling of being back home.

"Yes. Is that going to be too soon? I can't change the dates."

"It's fine. I'll be available."

"Posner was worried you wouldn't make it." Jake said.

"You can tell him I'll be there. I better go. I have company."

"Okay. Maybe I'll stop by later today."

"Probably not a good idea," I said.

"You ashamed of me?"

"Okay. You're weirding me out."

"I'm just hoping for a chance to pick up where we left off last night."

I felt my face get hot and was glad I wasn't face to face with him. "I'm not going to say I regret last night, but it was simply my libido getting the better of my brain. I wasn't expecting it and I've got other things on my mind."

"Embrace your libido, Alex. It'll make you a much happier person. Well, more fulfilled, anyway."

"I'll call you a little later."

I hung up without giving him the opportunity to say any more.

When I stepped out of my bedroom, Brown immediately asked if I had a job.

"Yeah, tomorrow."

"Good," Blue said. "You should stay busy. Can you talk about it?"

"It's just a security job for—"

"Another piece of shit security job? You're better than that, Alex." Brown said.

"What do you mean? If I still worked here, I'd be taking on security jobs."

"But we protect important people," he argued.

"So Angel isn't important?"

"It wasn't *her* you were protecting," he countered.

"The hell it wasn't."

"Whatever." He pouted.

"You better get down and see Gabriella before you go," Green cut in. "She should be in the office by now."

He set his cup in the kitchen sink.

"I've got things to do. See ya all later."

"We'll join you," Blue gave Brown a stern look as he followed Green to the door.

"I'll be right with you guys," Brown said. "Hold the elevator."

He waited until they were gone then said, "Alex. There are so many things I needed to say to Will. I'm not going to let that opportunity slide by with you."

He came close, but watched the floor as he spoke.

"You are a big part of me. I never thought you'd be gone as long as you were. Being here for coffee made me think you were back for good. You not being with the company wasn't something I ever thought about. I know you have issues with Red. Believe me, you aren't the only one. I don't think Blue has spoken to him since you left, and I've definitely given him a piece of my mind. But, if it takes us getting rid of Red to get you back, it's not going to happen.

"Yes, he needs a swift kick in the ass, but he's as important as you are. You are the one who left and he's the one who stayed. You decided your own fate, even if it was only to protect Red."

He looked up from the floor to confront me face to face.

"If you come back, you'll have more than just me in your corner. If you don't come back, you will still have more than just me in your corner. I guess, what I want to say is, we care about you outside of your ability to complete a job. Red does, too. I don't think he realized it until you left, but he really does."

His normal playful grin returned.

"Sometimes I wish you were a man. You would have kicked his ass and then the two of you would have pretended like none of this ever happened."

"Thanks, Brown," I said.

He nodded and left me alone in my apartment. I stood in the same spot for a long time. I didn't know what to do. I'd just gotten what I'd always wanted. The men asked me to come back. White let me know, in a roundabout way, he still loved me. But, I still resisted.

Why? Was I afraid of confronting Red?

No. I agreed with Brown. I should have kicked Red's ass. But, that wouldn't have ended it for me. Even if we'd talked this through before I left, I still wouldn't be okay with everything.

I'd been doing exactly what I wanted to do and with people I genuinely cared for. Then Red had changed up the game pieces and I didn't like it. My life was ripped away.

I'd been lured into believing I was on a level playing field, if not perching somewhere on the high ground, until this all went down. Now I felt like I was down in the sewers with no true friends. Their verbal claims just weren't good enough for me. I felt betrayed, and not by just Red.

I knew it wasn't quite as simple as this, but it fit well enough for my own personal understanding of my actions.

They'd tried to find me. White tried to keep in contact.

Those are all excuses in their favor.

I shouldn't have had to hide outside of the company. I should never have felt threatened from these men. Never. They were the people I relied on and I would die for them. Expecting them to back me in this situation was not asking too much.

I was pissed off beyond recovery. I had no idea how to fix that. Until I did, I couldn't work next to any of these men. I couldn't even consider it at the moment.

I called Jake and made a lunch date with him. He told me to get my bags ready and we'd drop them by the airport after lunch. We were taking a private jet, and it would be easiest to load up the cargo today.

"Okay," I said. "Can you meet me at the office? I need to say goodbye to Gabriella."

"No problem. See you soon."

Chapter Eighteen

GABRIELLA DIDN'T LOOK UP IMMEDIATELY from her computer screen when I walked into the office. I took the seat in front of her desk before she noticed me.

"Alex!"

She hurried around the desk and I stood to accept her hug.

"Your hair. It's grown so much since I saw you last."

She fiddled with my hair for a few seconds.

"You here because of Will?"

Tears formed in her eyes.

I nodded.

"You need to see White?"

She hiked her head toward the open office door.

I looked inside and saw White on the phone. One hand held the receiver, the other was pressed to his forehead.

"Yeah. I need to talk to him, but I can wait until he gets off the phone."

"Did you— I mean, are you coming back?"

"No."

"He didn't ask you to come back?" she whispered.

"Everyone but Red asked me to come back. I'm just not ready to admit defeat."

Her expression was confused.

"It's okay. Do you have a little time to visit before my ride for lunch shows up?" I asked.

"Of course I do. You need to fill me in on what's been going on."

"You first. I want to know about your wedding plans. Have they progressed at all?"

She held out her hand and showed me a gorgeous ring.

"Did you elope?" I grinned.

"Shhh."

She looked around the room as if there might be spies behind the filing cabinets.

"His mother doesn't know. Martin told her he'd let me wear the ring until we decided what we were going to do. His mother is set on a wedding. She knows it's her only chance at a wedding dress." She winked.

"Not if Leland finds himself feeling a bit flamboyant," I said.

"Nope. Leland and his partner have already done the dirty. Martin's mother was not pleased with that. At all."

"I thought you said the family was okay with Leland's orientation."

"Oh, not that part. She adores Stan. She was mad she didn't get to plan an elaborate wedding. So, now," she sighed, "Martin and I get to deal with that. Dealing with all the details was fun for a while, but I got to thinking about what you said. It's not about the ceremony, it's about me and Martin. I'd rather spend our money on other things."

"So, if you were willing to elope, why not tell her you'll compromise. Tell her you'll get married without all the fuss, but ask her to plan the reception and surprise you? I say, if it makes her happy, and you don't really care, let her do it."

"You know what? I'm going to suggest this to Martin tonight. That's a great idea. Now you have to tell me what you've been doing. It's been months, *again*."

"I quit working for my dad and started working for Mesa. Kind of quit working for them and am now freelance. I have a job tomorrow. I'll be gone three months for this one."

"You aren't going to stay here with White?"

She actually looked offended.

"He'll be fine without me."

I looked into his office. He'd gotten off the phone and had turned his chair to face the window. Now it was my turn for my eyes to fill with tears.

"Honey. I'm sure he'll be just fine. You do what you have to."

"He's off the phone. I should go in and say my goodbyes."
I left Gabriella at her desk and shut White's door
behind me.

"Hi," I said as he turned his chair to face me.

"Been on the phone all morning with your dad," he said.

"About what?"

"He won't give me the report on Will's death." White was
obviously frustrated and drained.

"I'd offer to try to convince him, but he's not even talking
to me right now."

"We're both in a hell-of-a mess, aren't we."

I nodded. "I've got a job. I leave tomorrow."

"With Jake?"

"For Mesa," I answered.

He sighed. "Alex—" His gaze was intense. He stared at
me for maybe five seconds before he sighed and shook his
head. "Asking as a friend," he said. "Can you tell me about
the job?"

"I haven't been told to not talk about it. I'll be a guard at
a South American refinery for three months."

"Three months. Will you be coming back to your apartment when you get back?"

"Probably," I said.

"So, you've been to see Gabriella in the past couple
months?" He moved from behind his desk to stand directly
in front of me.

"How'd you know that?"

White reached over and took my hair between his fingers. "She touched your hair and said it had grown. How short did you cut your hair?"

"About this short." I waved my fingers just below my ears.

"Bet it looked nice. Not that I don't like it now," he said. "But, I like it long, too."

"What does this have to do with anything?"

"Nothing. Just thought I'd make a comment on your hair since it's different. It looks nice."

"Thanks."

He held my gaze. I could clearly see the pain in his eyes and had to fight to hold my head up.

"Alex." He caressed my cheek with the back of his hand. "I'll always be here for you, even if you can't bring yourself to come back to the company. I just want you to know that."

I couldn't speak and I couldn't keep eye contact any more, either. Last night, with Jake, slapped me in the face.

"I'm sorry, White." I took a step backward. I'd been an idiot and let my hormones get the best of me. Last night was one of the biggest mistakes I'd ever made. I sickened myself. White deserved better.

"It's okay. I thought about what you said last night, and you were right. But, I'm still not going to make an active decision. It's up to you now. You can come back to work at any time. But, that means working with Red. He's killed off Penumbra, so I can't imagine he'd have anything worth talking about. I suspect, if you gave him a chance, he could make it up to you."

I snorted and shook my head.

"I know," he said. "I don't mean to sound like I'm minimizing anything. I'm not. No one has. Something that might bring you a little satisfaction; Red's been off the books since you left. I've not given him any jobs and I've not met any resistance for my decision from any of the partners."

"What? You've cut him off?"

"And he's not complained, either. He knows, Alex."

This revelation made my pride swell a little.

"I'll keep in touch after I get back," I said.

"Good. We miss you and we need you." He went back to his chair behind his desk. "Something else I think you should know, before you come back," he added. "The Admiral has cut our job allotment by more than half. I'm sure he's done this because you're no longer an active member of the company."

"I'm so sorry, Rick," I said.

"No."

He held up a hand and shook his head.

"It was expected and we're still doing just fine. I just didn't want you to find out about it later and think that's the only reason I'm asking you to come back to us. It's not. In fact, if you do come back and he starts offering more jobs, I'll probably decline most of them. I'm sorry to say, but he's been a major pain in my ass since you left."

"Rick. I'll keep in touch, but I don't know if I'm coming back to the company. I have to think about that more." I looked at my watch. Jake would be here soon and I decided it probably wasn't such a good idea to put the two men together. I didn't think Jake had any intentions of a long-term relationship with me, but men were funny about their conquests. I knew White wasn't sure about us. I wasn't sure we could salvage anything. That could cause some friction and White didn't need that. The loss of Will was still very raw.

"I better get going. I have to meet someone for lunch. You really should consider going to the service your parents have planned," I said.

"No. My grief is mine. I don't have to show them how much I'm going to miss Will to actually miss him."

I nodded my understanding.

"So, you'll be back here, but not necessarily back to work?"

Again, I nodded.

"What about us?" he asked.

My voice caught in my throat, so I just shrugged. I didn't want to break down in front of him. I wanted nothing more than to be back in his arms. I wanted to walk up to him right this second and kiss him full on the lips. But I felt dirty after kissing Jake. White really did deserve better.

Finally, I spoke. "You might be better off without me."

"I'm not going to ask you to explain yourself. I just want you to be happy." He pushed the button on his intercom.

"Gabriella, would you send Mr. Jensen in please?" He took his finger off the button.

I was shocked. When had Jake gotten here and how did White know he was here? He'd not taken any calls since I came in.

"I'll see you in three months. Be careful." He dismissed me.

I reached the door at the same time Jake opened it and stepped in.

"I won't be long," he said as I passed him.

GABRIELLA'S EXPRESSION WAS QUESTIONING. "YOU work for him?" she asked.

"Yes."

"Damn, girl. You sure know how to pick 'em."

Gabriella's voice made me tear my eyes from White's closed office door.

"I just work with him."

"You can't tell me you haven't thought about that in your bed," she said. "He's *fine*."

I shrugged. "He's okay, I guess."

"Okay? You're hedging. You've already been there." She was so sure of herself.

"No. I haven't, actually."

My stomach was in knots, wondering what they were talking about in White's office and Gabriella wasn't making this any easier for me.

"But you want to."

"All I want, right now, is to know what they are talking about in there."

"Ha," Gabriella said. "I can imagine. If I hear anything break, I'm calling Black."

I strained my ears and Gabriella must have done the same because she didn't keep talking.

After two minutes of quiet, Gabriella said, "Sit down, Alex. Your pacing is making me seasick."

"Sorry." I sat down and caught myself leaning forward, trying to hear something come from the office.

Gabriella sat much the same way I did, obviously straining to hear something, too.

"It's no use," she said. "No matter how hard I try, I've never heard anything come from his office after the door was shut. As long as the conversation remained civil."

Just then, White's door opened. He stood on the threshold and shook Jake's hand before he let him pass. Then he looked directly at me and gave me a wan smile and a slight nod of his head.

I cocked my head in a question, but he just went back into his office and shut the door behind him. "What was that about?" I asked.

"Uh." Jake looked at Gabriella then back at me. "Nothing," he said.

I shook my head.

"No. That's not going to cut it."

"You really want to talk about this now?"

"You're damn right she wants to talk about it now," Gabriella said.

"He threatened me. I threatened him. We shook on it." Jake shrugged. "You ready to go to lunch now?"

I looked at Gabriella.

"I can live with that," she said.

"Fine. Let's go," I answered Jake.

When we got on the elevator I told Jake to repeat his conversation with White verbatim.

He looked up at the camera deliberately. "We'll talk in the car."

"Fine." I hurried through the lobby with Jake struggling to keep up.

"It's not a race, Alex," he said.

"Shut up and get your ass out here."

I held the door open to the garage.

"I parked on the street. They wouldn't let me into the garage."

"Damn it."

I let the door slide shut and made my way to the front doors.

As soon as we were in the car, I demanded to hear the conversation.

"Alex. I'm not going to repeat it word for word. What I told you in the office is what I thought Gabriella would like to hear."

"So you didn't threaten each other."

"No. He asked me about a few jobs we've done lately. He keeps an eye on Posner, and I oblige with a little information here and there. Where do you want to go for lunch?"

"You pick. I'm not hungry."

"Come on, Alex. What did you expect? Even if we both have an interest in what only one of us can have, doesn't mean we don't still have real jobs."

"Good," I said.

My ego was bruised, but I was sincerely relieved I wasn't going to be an item of contention between them. I loved White and didn't want to cause him any hurt. And, I had feelings for Jake, too. I didn't want to hurt him, either.

He laughed. "I didn't mean to make you feel inferior. I'm certainly not going to object to sex with you. Sex is fine with me. Last night was fun, but I won't fight White for you. You come willingly or you don't come at all. Simple as that. I sure as hell am not going to jeopardize my standing with White, of all people, to get you in my bed."

Again, another slam to my ego. At least now I knew where I stood with him. It made things much easier for me.

"Just shut up and drive."

He did as he was told and when we got to the restaurant I went straight to the bathroom. My pride was hurt, but I was glad I hadn't been the topic. I just wished Jake hadn't made it clear he was only in it for the sex. If it had gone any further last night, I would be devastated.

After taking a minute to compose myself, I found Jake's table and joined him.

"You aren't going to like this," he said as he picked at the bread at the table.

"What?"

"We leave right after lunch. Not tomorrow."

"What's with the change in plans? I already told everyone I was leaving tomorrow."

"Something with the boat scheduling. Just got the call. You still in?"

"Yes." I sighed.

Chapter Nineteen

ABOUT AN HOUR LATER, I found myself on a private jet with Jake, Joe, and Eric. Eric glared at me for the first couple hours of the flight, but I pretended I didn't notice and sat quietly in my seat.

Less than a day later I found myself on a small yacht, floating lazily down the river. My conscience nagged at me as I came out on deck. I'd actually forgotten about the fishing trip and it grated on me. I should have stayed with White and flown down after the vacation was over and the job had begun.

I slumped down in a chair and opened a book. I struggled with my feelings of guilt for leaving White to go fishing for a few days before the job. There was nothing I could do about it now, so I tried to concentrate on the book.

Jake, Eric, and Joe fished from the back deck and didn't seem to notice me right away. I had a little trouble turning the pages on my book. They were floppy and sticky because of the high humidity, but I kept trying. Reading was my escape, but today it was my nemesis.

Having so much trouble turning the pages just added to my annoyance, so I watched the guys fish. They were having a good time bantering with each other and had finally noticed me in my chair. Every once in a while they tried to include me. Eric was the most persistent, and becoming even more resolute with every drink he had. Eventually, Eric hobbled toward my comfortable deck chair using his fishing pole as a crutch.

"What's this?" Eric grabbed my book. "We aren't out here to watch you read. You either fish or you get off the boat."

I doubted his broken nose was healed, his eyes still had some unnatural color to the lids. By the way he grabbed my book, he must not have broken his hand when he threw that punch into the wall.

I recognized the anger in his eyes. He played it off as if he was joking, but he was still pissed about his knee. I didn't take the bait and held my hand out for my book. His top lip curled up and he tossed the book out into the river.

I kept my calm and left my hand out.

"Go get it yourself."

"Fishing pole?" I said.

Eric grinned, but he wasn't happy. He'd really wanted a fight this morning. Still, he handed over his pole. When I took hold of the pole I also took hold of his wrist. I flipped around him and pushed him down on his face. I stepped in the middle of his back and held his arm straight up with one hand on his wrist and the other on his elbow. If I kept up the pressure there was no way Eric could wriggle out of his current position.

I bent down and replaced my foot with my knee.

"Here's the fight you were aching for. You still wanna play? I'm warning you, I don't play well with others, lately. Thought you might have learned your lesson back at Mesa." I felt my top lip curl, mimicking Eric's previous expression. I welcomed it. It felt good to get the best of him again.

"Get off me," he growled.

"I don't like you, Eric. If it wasn't clear, it should be now. Just for the record, I don't care who you are to Posner. There is no way I'm going to allow you to push me around. I'm better than you. Simple as that."

"Hey!" Jake's voice filtered into my ears. "What the hell is going on?"

I waited for him to reach us before I jumped up and away from Eric. As soon as I let go, Eric got up and lunged for me. I was expecting it and popped him in the mouth. I didn't hit him hard enough to draw blood, but I did stop him in his tracks.

Jake stepped between us and glared. "I don't want to babysit the whole trip. Get over it. We have a job to do. I can't afford to have you two trying to kill each other when we might have a real enemy to fight."

He waited for both of us to nod our understanding before he continued.

"We're all going out on the boat," Jake said as he indicated one of the small fishing boats moored at the back of the yacht.

"Might as well," I said.

The four of us fished the remainder of the day. I kept as much distance between myself and Eric as I possibly could on that small boat. He never showed me any further animosity. Eventually, we caught up to the yacht that had anchored downriver for the night. Jake explained the yacht would anchor every night so we'd be able to pick up our fishing where we left off every morning until we reached the docks of the refinery a few days from now.

The next couple of days proceeded the same way until we pulled up near shore after the yacht had rounded a bend early that morning.

"Here's your stop," Eric said.

"What do you mean?"

"You get off here. This pack has water, a few supplies, a map and a compass. If you can reach the refinery, you'll be put on the crew." He shoved a pack at me.

I looked at Jake for support and he just shrugged.

"Initiation process," he said.

"Fine." I took the pack and jumped from the small boat. This wasn't my first time in the wilderness alone. But, it was my first time in the jungle alone.

I stepped into the trees before the boat left the shore. When I was sure I was no longer visible to the men on the boat I opened my pack. They certainly didn't leave me much. I found everything they'd listed as well as a survival knife and machete.

I pulled White's cell phone from my back pocket. It had been shut off so Jake wouldn't know I'd brought it along. I'd been considering getting rid of the phone for so many months. It was always nice to be reminded of the practical reason I kept it. I switched it on and coordinated my location and that of the refinery. If I pushed hard, I might even make the refinery before the men who'd thrown me overboard.

I studied the map for a couple minutes longer making sure to mark the landmarks in my mind so I wouldn't have to stop until dark.

After an hour of hiking through the heavy brush I was exhausted. The humidity clung to me, and sweat dripped from the end of my nose. I stopped to check my map and take a short breather.

I took in my surroundings as I studied the map again. This was nothing like the mountains where White and Associates had their cabin. The vegetation was so thick I couldn't see more than a few feet in any direction. I was more thankful for the machete than even the water in my pack.

I hadn't strayed too far from the river bank and the voices of men picked their way across the thick air. I'd caught up to the fishing buddies. They bantered back and forth as if they hadn't just stranded a woman out in the jungle not much more than an hour before.

I slowly made my way closer to the river so I could catch a glimpse of my current enemies. It was almost impossible to be quiet moving through the vegetation so my advance was slow and their voices drifted further downstream.

White's phone vibrated in my back pocket and I let out a quick yelp.

"Follow the river and you'll eventually make the docks," I heard Eric's voice.

His acknowledgement of my presence pissed me off and I moved further from the river in response.

I pulled out the phone and dialed White. The phone didn't connect. I must not have signal, but why had it vibrated?

"Damn it." I said.

I'd set up a few alarms and since I'd been keeping the phone off most of the time, I'd forgotten about them. I just shut the phone off again. I didn't want to take the time to play around with my phone right now.

A few minutes later I stopped to check the map. The river snaked its way through the jungle and a straight line would, hopefully, serve me better than following the water. There was one spot where the river branched around a large island. It threatened to add ten or fifteen miles to my straight path unless I could somehow cross the river. Depending on how wide it was, I might chance a dip in the water.

I pushed hard into the jungle for several more hours. My inability to remain quiet in this setting was getting to me. I decided this was the perfect opportunity to work on my stealth. If I could master being quiet in this tangle, I should be able to sneak up on almost anything.

I found I could be quiet, but the time it took was just too much. Besides, I'd seen plenty of snakes, spiders and other wildlife, maybe letting them know I was coming through wasn't such a bad idea. It would give them the chance to move out of my path instead of making me stop dead in my tracks. I'd already come up on a couple of snakes and I'd been lucky enough to see them before stepping on one and another one had been on a branch right at eye level. I almost had a face full of possible poisonous snake. I'd still have to avoid the spiderwebs made of thinly spun steel, and brush the bugs from my arms, neck, and forehead. But, I could move faster if I didn't worry about my noise level.

The thick tree trunks seemed to cluster closer together as the sun's light started to fail. I was not looking forward to sleeping out here with all these critters in such close proximity, but it couldn't be helped. All I could do was pray I wouldn't get malaria.

I was within a quarter of a mile of a bend in the river and I decided to try to make it as close as I could. Despite the noise I'd made crashing through the jungle, I was pleased with my progress. I was thankful I hadn't followed the river. If I had, I'd still be several miles from my current location. It was possible I'd made better time than the yacht.

I slowed as I came closer to the water. The trees thinned a little and I realized the sun wasn't as close to setting as I'd thought. Jake, Joe, and Eric might still be out on their little boat fishing to their hearts content.

My pace continued to decrease as I came even closer to the bank of the river and I could hear voices once again. Finally, I was able to see the water and the yacht wasn't far. The fishing boat was nowhere to be seen, so I decided to try my luck.

"Hey!" I yelled across to the captain and waved my arms.

"Miss. Are you okay?"

"Yes. Can I board?"

"Of course."

He was already pointing another member of his crew to the remaining fishing boat. Within ten minutes I found myself grabbing the captain's hand to steady myself as I boarded.

"Thank you."

"Is everything okay, miss?"

"Yes. Everything is fine. I was wondering if there was any way I could move down the river much faster than our current pace. I'd like to reach our final destination as soon as possible."

"Of course. I can have one of my men take you down river in the other fishing boat."

"How long will that take?"

"He can have you there in a couple hours."

I sighed.

"We're really that close?"

"Yep."

"When do you expect the rest of my party to get back to the yacht?"

"I don't expect to see them until right before dark."

He must have seen the question looming on my lips. "In about three or four hours," he added.

"Is there any way we can keep this arrangement from the men in my group?"

"Of course, miss. May I ask why? You aren't in trouble, are you?"

"No, Captain. Everything is just fine. They just thought it would be character building to make me hike to our destination."

He grinned. "Is the jungle not to your liking?"

"It's beautiful, but not easy to move through. I was not looking forward to fending off the insects or crocodiles for the next several days. You've saved me a lot of trouble."

"The jungle really isn't a good place for a young woman on her own. You go collect your things and I'll make sure the boat is equipped for night travel."

Then he cleared his throat.

"I hope you are able to compensate me for the loss of two men from my crew for your trip."

"I have some money, how much do you require?"

I didn't haggle for very long because I wanted to be long gone before the men came in from their day of fishing. Still, the price was definitely worth not having to beat my way through the jungle for the next several days and to keep the captain from telling the men how I'd gotten so far ahead of them.

Ten minutes later I handed the cash to the captain, my bags to a crew member on the fishing boat, and accepted a hand from another man to help me aboard.

The captain stood counting the money as we piloted away from the yacht.

Chapter Twenty

T HE RIDE IN THE FISHING boat was uneventful and quiet, except for the outboard motor. Within two hours I could see concrete walls of the refinery looming a short distance away. The place was a fortress.

As our little fishing boat pulled up next to the barge moored to the dock, one of the men tossed my bags out.

"Hurry," he told me.

The source of his unease was obvious. A group of armed men were coming from the refinery gates to greet us.

I stepped from the boat and looked around. The refinery's high wall boasted towers every few hundred feet, or so. Each of the towers were manned with two armed guards. I could tell more armed men walked the wall because I could see them briefly pass by open slots in the thick walls. I assumed the openings were for defense reasons. The trees had been cleared away from the premises several hundred feet.

My ride left the dock and went back the way we'd come.

"What do you want?" the man heading up the welcoming committee demanded as he took a defensive stance, aiming his AR-15 directly at my head. The other five men all followed his lead. If I wasn't careful, I might spring several leaks right quick.

I kept my voice even and said, "Alex Grey. I'm here with Jake Jensen's crew."

"Where's Jake?"

I hiked my head back toward the river. "Still fishing."

He relaxed his stance only somewhat before he gave a commanding jerk of his head indicating I should move his way. I reached down to grab my duffle bags.

"Leave 'em!" he commanded.

I moved back to an upright position with my hands held at shoulder height. These guys were very jumpy. I thought this was supposed to be a leisurely security job. Jake had told me nothing much ever happened because everyone knew the place was well-guarded.

The man instructed three of the guards behind him to come get me. My machete was immediately taken from me. One of them carefully opened my bags and rummaged through them while the other two stepped behind me and trained their weapons on my back.

"Just normal stuff, Bud," the man finally reported.

"Pat her down," he ordered.

I assumed the position and endured the sweeping motions across my shoulders and down my arms, but flinched when he moved to my lower back. He lifted my shirt and pulled out my six shot Beretta. He checked the safety, ejected the magazine, and cleared the chamber. He slid it down the dock toward the man giving the orders. The search continued until he found the matching Beretta in my ankle holster. As soon as he secured that pistol he slid it down the dock to join its partner.

"Anything else?" he asked me when he finished the basic sweep.

Somehow, he missed the survival knife I had on a chain around my neck and White's cell phone I'd hidden as deeply as I could in my front left pocket. I guess he was being polite by not fondling my lady parts.

"Nope," I assured him.

"That's it, Bud," he told his boss.

"Carry her bags. Let's go."

One of the men behind me nudged me with the barrel of his rifle and we all walked down the dock and through the gate of the refinery.

We marched directly toward a building about three hundred feet to the left of the gate.

They escorted me inside and placed me in a cell-like room. It had dingy gray walls with a grimy-looking cot and a toilet in one corner.

"If your story checks out, we'll be back for you. But, if you're lying you might as well get comfortable," the man called Bud said.

The door was shut firmly and I was left alone in the dark room. There were no windows, so the only light came in through the small crack at the bottom of the door.

I pulled out the phone and turned it on for a little light. I was thankful the guard hadn't been more frisky with his weapons search.

A quick sweep of the room showed no weaknesses I could exploit with a knife and a cell phone, at least none other than the actual doorknob. I was sure I could pry it off with my knife, but I decided I'd wait it out. The bottom of the door, where the light filtered in, was actually a slot. I imagined that was how they got food and water to the prisoners.

I hoped Jake and the guys would be at the refinery by tomorrow.

I tried to get comfortable on the bare mattress, but it smelled like old sweat. I decided to curl up on the cool cement floor instead.

I woke up to a numb hip. Cement wasn't as forgiving as dirt. I wondered how long I'd slept. Again, I turned on the phone, but to check the time instead of for the light. My eyes had adjusted to the darkness and I could make out everything in the room from the meager light coming under the door.

I'd slept for ten hours. No wonder my hip was numb. Staying on my side for that long on a comfortable mattress would probably have the same consequences.

Jake, Eric, and Joe should be at the refinery in a few hours, this afternoon, at the latest.

About fifteen minutes later, I found myself pacing my room. What the hell was I going to do until they decided to let me out?

Relax. What's a few hours of down time? You can handle this.

I kept talking myself down from the panic that wanted to well up.

My thoughts were all over the place. Was I really a prisoner? Everyone had warned me about working with Mesa, even if they hadn't given me a clear reason. Maybe this wasn't a test, maybe this was real.

When do I decide they are actually holding me and not testing me? Mesa hadn't really tested me the way White and Associates had, but that didn't mean I thought they weren't going to.

Was Jake pissed off at me for some reason? Maybe Eric had this planned and since Posner was always on his side, I'd never get out.

I'd been told the Admiral and Posner had a running animosity toward each other. What if Posner had found out I was the Admiral's daughter? Maybe he was trying to get even with my dad.

I had to force myself to leave the phone in my pocket for fear of running down the battery by checking the time every few minutes. At least I had a signal here. If it came down to it, I could call for help. That was one good thing. I was almost certain my ex-partners would save me, if I needed them to. I'd have to be sure I was in real danger first, though.

At one point, someone came to the door and shoved in a tray of food. A bottle of water rolled in after the tray.

After the slot was closed, I used my phone to check out the grub. It looked edible, so I gave it a try. It wasn't bad, but it was the water that was the most appealing. Then I checked the time since I already had the phone on. It had only been an hour since I woke up. How was I going to make it till this afternoon? And, that was assuming they'd let me out when Jake showed up.

I guessed it was maybe five minutes later when the slot opened up again and a voice demanded I slide the tray and water bottle back out of the room.

I did what was asked of me after I guzzled down the rest of the water. The hatch slammed back down as soon as the water bottle rolled back through.

This played out again around dinner time. I didn't even realize they'd skipped lunch, leaving my afternoon deadline in the dust, until I used the light from the phone to check the time. As I ate, I decided to wait it out a little longer.

They fed me once again the next morning. Finally, by the time it opened up again for another dinner, I'd made up my mind. I wouldn't stay another day in this cell.

I got to work on the doorknob almost as soon as I'd pushed the remains of my dinner and water bottle back through the slat. Thankfully, the door was wooden and not metal. Within an hour I had the knob loose.

Just a little bit more.

I was right. Just a little bit more and the knob fell off and into my hands. But, the knob on the other side of the door didn't have a pair of hands to fall into. It clanged to the floor with an awful sound.

Shit.

My adrenaline level escalated. I could feel my heart beat inside my chest, my breathing seemed overly loud, and my hands wanted to shake. I looked through the hole in the door, but didn't see anyone investigating the sound. Still, the door wouldn't open.

Crap.

I didn't know if it was my adrenaline, the hours I'd spent fretting over every single possibility, or my anger at being locked up, but all I wanted now was to get out.

I imagined they had some sort of deadbolt on the out-side of the door. I changed my tactics and went to work on the hinges instead. Since the clatter of the fallen knob hadn't alerted anyone, I took a chance and worked as fast as I could instead of as quietly as I could. After some prying, I had the hinges off the door and pushed it open. The padlocked latch was all that kept the door from slamming to the floor.

I heard a groan from a nearby cell. This only added to my unease. Who the hell would they be keeping locked up? The man's voice was muffled and dry-sounding. Knowing they actually kept prisoners bothered me. I wondered again who they'd keep locked up. I considered checking the cells, but what would I do with the prisoners, and maybe they should be locked up. I had no way to know.

I couldn't believe they didn't have anyone standing guard inside the building. That didn't mean they didn't have someone nearby. It seemed like they had a well-run place when they captured me a couple days ago.

I still didn't know what I was going to do after I left the building. I was at the mercy of these people. Trying to make it to civilization through the jungle wasn't a good option.

Where the hell was Jake?

I found my equipment near the front door of the building in a heap. I equipped my pistols and slung the bags onto my shoulder.

I wasn't sure of my options. Did I really need to escape? If I did, I wouldn't spare anyone who got in my way. But, if I was going to work with these people I probably shouldn't run around the refinery killing them.

I rummaged through my bags, found my other phone, and dialed Jake.

"Alex?" His voice carried surprise.

"Are you here at the refinery?"

"Yes. How'd you get your phone?"

"So, you did know I was in a holding cell."

"Of course I did. You cheated and got a ride to the refinery. It's your punishment."

The sense of relief I should have felt after hearing Jake's voice and his explanation was absent. I wasn't convinced I didn't need to protect myself, but the intensity of my paranoia was pushed down under the rage.

"I'm done being punished. I have no idea if what you say is true, but I'm walking out of this building right now. If I'm met with any resistance I will respond with serious intent. You better inform your men to stand down or shoot to kill, because I won't miss and I'm armed."

I hung up the phone and placed it in my back pocket. After a deep breath, I made sure the safety was off on both pistols, and made sure I had one in each chamber. Then, I threw open the door.

I found the guard. He was positioned right outside the door and it had hit him hard when I flung it open. I'd stunned him, but he was fumbling for his rifle.

"Drop it!" I ordered.

I could tell he was gauging my mood. He picked the right choice and lifted the gun strap off his neck and dropped the rifle.

I replaced one pistol to my back holster and trained the second on him.

"On the ground. Face first, hands behind your back." I said calmly.

Again, he complied. I retrieved his rifle and stowed my remaining pistol into my ankle holster. I took advantage of the FlexiCuffs on his belt and secured his hands behind his back.

"Get up," I instructed.

As he stood, I heard a voice come over his radio instructing all men to stand down. Still, the men in the towers surrounding us had kept their attention inward as well as the men who walked the wall.

I stood behind him with the rifle trained on his back and waited. It wasn't long before Jake, Eric, Joe, and Bud came into view about fifty yards away. None of them were carrying weapons.

"Alex," Jake called across the distance. "You can drop the weapon."

I wanted to, but I felt like a trapped animal. Even though the small crowd approaching me on the ground was unarmed, I was well aware of the men in the towers who'd trained their weapons on me.

"Am I going to be issued better accommodations?"

"Of course."

The guys stopped about twenty feet from me.

"Have your tower crews drop their weapons and I'll consider dropping mine."

Jake gave me a sly smile.

"I thought you trusted me." He told Bud to tell the men to stand down.

Bud didn't hesitate to speak the order into his radio and the men in the towers complied. I pushed my prisoner forward and lowered my weapon.

Bud cut the bonds off the guard and told him to find his rack for the night.

"What's with the show of force?" Eric sneered.

"What's with keeping me in that cell?" I imitated his expression and raised the rifle again. Eric would be the first.

"Give me the rifle, Alex." Jake reached out.

I took a step backward.

"Guys, I'll meet you back at headquarters in a few," Jake said to the rest of the men.

They took the hint and left us alone.

Jake stood in front of me quietly until the men were out of sight.

"How'd you get out?"

"My knife."

"They were supposed to have taken everything from you."

"The guard who frisked me was a gentleman." I was starting to calm down.

"We can't have any of that," Jake said. He smiled broadly.

"You have a door to fix." I hiked my head back to the prison.

Jake laughed. "Come on. I'll take you to your room. I made sure you were next door to me instead of in the barracks."

We walked in the direction Joe and the rest of the men had gone. I still carried the rifle.

"You want to know the funny part of all this?" Jake asked.

"What's that?"

"I was just about to come get you."

"You should have come before dinner," I said.

We'd made our way deeper into the refinery. I was surrounded by large, round holding tanks, so the large rectangular buildings in the middle of them looked out of place. Yet, they softened the industrial feel somewhat by adding a touch of humanity.

We walked toward the three-story building in the middle of the shorter buildings.

"This is what we call headquarters. It's where the main office for the refinery is, so it sees a lot of traffic. It's also where the higher ranking officers, like us, and the foremen bunk. It also houses a place for all employees to eat and socialize. The buildings on either side are the barracks. The two on the left are for the employees and the one on the right is for our guys, the security."

We walked into the building and were met immediately with men milling around a large central room. It held arcade games, a small bar, several long tables, and televisions.

Joe, Eric, and Bud were seated at the long table nearest the door. The room quieted almost as soon as Jake and I entered and all eyes were on us. Actually, they were all on me and the rifle I still carried.

Let 'em come take it from me.

I'd give anyone in this room a good fight. It looked like most of them were refinery workers and not security. But, the ones who were obviously security would still have a hell of a fight on their hands. I had the weapon.

Eric started to approach us. I held the rifle a little closer and I watched Jake motion him back with a slight hand movement.

"Our rooms are on the next floor."

Jake lightly put his hand on my shoulder. I cringed and held the rifle a little tighter.

"Whoa. Being in that cell really got to you. I'm not going to hurt you."

He must have thought I might go on a shooting spree. Honestly, if anyone approached me too quickly or aggressively, I might. I didn't realize how much I hadn't liked being cooped up for two days in the dark. I wanted to let the tension drop away, but I just couldn't. I was a walking bag of paranoia at the moment.

Jake and I rode the elevator up a floor in silence.

"This way." He led me down the hall to the left of the elevator after we stepped out. The door he opened was only a few feet down the hall. I followed him inside.

"This is my room. You're next door." He pointed to the open doors that joined the two rooms.

"Adjoining rooms? Isn't that a bit presumptuous?"

"Not at all. If I had presumed anything we'd be in the same room, sharing a bed."

He winked.

I walked into my room and dropped my bags onto the chair near the desk.

I stood the rifle up in the corner, near the front door, before I started going through my things.

Jake watched me from our shared door. I gave a slight jump when he asked, "You okay?"

"I'm fine." I made sure the rifle was still in its place before I asked, "You want the rifle back?"

"Eventually." He shrugged. "I'm in no hurry. If it makes you feel better, keep it. I had a similar reaction to my isolation training," he said.

"That was not isolation training. That was bullshit."

"You weren't supposed to catch a ride. You were supposed to navigate your way through the jungle."

"You didn't give me any rules. You just pushed me out of the boat. I shouldn't be punished for finding my way to my destination before you could get here."

"Your logic makes sense, I guess. Next time, I'll be sure to state the rules before dumping you out of the boat."

"I will never allow you to lock me up again. Never." My voice was firm.

"Noted." He moved to my side and started to rub my shoulders. "Had I known you were claustrophobic I wouldn't have done that to you without some warning."

I shook his hands off and sat on the edge of the bed. "I'm not claustrophobic. What I am is unsure of *you*. I've enjoyed working with you. I'd like to keep up a good relationship with Mesa. But I've been told to be leery of Mesa at every turn, then I find myself in a cell. My mind was all over the place. It still is."

"We decided you should have to undergo the same initiation we've all gone through. You didn't. You caught a ride, so we decided to let you sweat it out in a cell for a couple days."

"I've already gone through the phase of proving myself. I won't do it again. You either take me as I am or you don't. I really don't give a shit. I told you once, I'm not going to kiss anyone's ass. I'm not here out of any obligation or any need. I'm here to keep a gun in my hands and working a job I was made for. I need to work, not be tested over and over again by people I don't want to prove myself to."

I sagged onto the bed and put my head in my hands. Jake's sudden weight on the mattress upset my balance and resulted in my body leaning into his. The physical attraction was still there for me, but I resisted and moved away from him.

"You have nothing to prove to me," he said.

"Then why put me in that damn cell? I'm already on edge. I can't trust anyone and you've proven that once again."

"You can trust me," he sounded offended.

I laughed. "That's what's got me into trouble. Trusting people like you."

"This work revolves around trust. If you can't trust me to have your back, you're out here all alone, and you won't come out on top," he said as he scooted closer to me again.

I stood up and away from his grasp. Those couple days in a holding cell had scared the crap out of me. I didn't want to be held against my will, ever. Jake's declaration that this job required trust was exactly right.

I paced for about thirty seconds. Trust was my main issue. With my background of being Penumbra, being my father's daughter, and my mother's daughter, I couldn't trust anyone. I'd thought I could trust my partners, but now I knew I couldn't.

I'd felt guilt for holding back my alternate personality. I'd thought they *should* know, until they found out. Now I knew the Admiral and White had good reason for keeping it secret. They knew they couldn't trust anyone, at least not completely. Not even their own partners. But, I did trust them more than anyone else and they'd told me to be careful working at Mesa.

I couldn't find any specific reason for their concern, but I knew there had to be a reason. I'd been ignoring their warnings because I wanted to fit in somewhere. Penumbra didn't fit in any group, she was an outsider. Even if I'd never do jobs as her again, I was still her. There was no getting past that fact. I had to protect my background at all costs and getting close to Jake or anyone else was not an option. White had been my only option in that department and that hadn't worked out too well.

"No matter how hard I try, I don't fit in anywhere. I'm killing time until I can go back to what I was doing before," I said.

"Working for White and Associates? You're definitely going back then?"

"No. Not White and Associates."

What was it about Jake that made me run off at the mouth?

"What then?"

I shook my head. I'd said too much and didn't know how to get out of this one.

"What did you do, Alex?" His look had become sly.

"Solitary jobs," I answered.

"What, like hit jobs? Is that why you told Posner you wouldn't take on any hit jobs? You were trying to get away from it? Cuz, Danny— No wonder you didn't hesitate."

"What about Danny?"

"That was a setup. Posner wanted him dead and we made sure you'd take the shot."

Now he'd said too much.

"Really? How did you set that up?"

My mind went back to the job and I relived my concern that Eric did nothing to help Jake after Danny had gotten his gun. I was furious, but I managed to keep my voice calm.

"I made sure Danny would get my gun. It wasn't loaded."

"So, I shot an unarmed man?"

"It's not like that, Alex. He'd used the company several times for his drug deals and Posner couldn't allow it any more. He wasn't going to be stopped any other way."

"Sure he would've. It was only a matter of time before the people he was double-crossing caught up with him. Besides, if Posner knew he was using the company for drug deals, why did he keep taking on the jobs?"

The memory of the dealers leaving in our SUV and Jake and Eric leaving in theirs came back to me. They were working with the dealers. The people Danny was double-crossing *did* catch up to him, and I was their weapon. No wonder I was told to be careful of Mesa. They were involved in some serious bad guy behavior.

Now I was, too.

Jake opened his mouth, but I held up my hand.

"I don't want to hear it. Save your breath." I shook my head in disgust. "I didn't take on hit jobs, until Danny. I was in data retrieval," I lied.

"Data retrieval? What do you mean?"

"It doesn't matter. I'm done talking to you. You set me up to kill a man, Jake."

"A man who deserved it," he said.

"Nevertheless. I should have been brought in on it."

"Would you have done the job?"

"No."

"We needed to know if you had it in you," he explained like it was nothing.

"Well, now you know. And you've been telling me to trust you? What else have you lied to me about?"

"Nothing else like that."

"What else?"

"I can't say. But what I can say is, you've passed every test, so far. Except the White and Associates test. You need to cut ties, Alex."

I laughed. "No way in hell are you going to tell me to cut ties with anyone."

"It's not me, it's Posner. This is going to be the last job offered unless you do."

"Then this will be my last job. In fact, if you can get me the hell out of here, I won't even work this one."

"Stick with me through this one. I'm sorry if I pissed you off. I just wanted you to know what kind of jobs you've been doing. I should have told you a long time ago, but I couldn't. I still can't tell you everything. I just wanted you to know I understand your distrust and it's not misplaced. Just know that you can trust *me*. I'll always have your back in a fight. But, there are certain things expected of me and I have to follow orders or risk my own life."

"Are you saying Posner would have you killed if you didn't follow orders?"

"I'm sure of it," he said.

I hadn't forgiven him for lying to me, but I understood it a little better.

"I'm actually playing both sides of the coin here, Alex. And, I need your help. I've been told that Posner might be in for a hard fall. If that's the case, I'm in a position to take over Mesa. All I need to do is bide my time, and I'd like to have you by my side, if push comes to shove with Eric."

"Is this why you're telling me all of this? You want me in your corner when it comes to Eric?"

"I've been waiting for the right time and this talk of trust— I thought now might be a good time to let you know you can trust me."

"Not a very good way to go about it."

I shook my head.

"That, and I've promised White a little more than I should have. But, if you happen to stumble across something while you're here, you can report back to him."

"What? Is this what you and White talked about in his office?"

"A little bit. I told him I'd put you in a position to help his cause."

"What is his cause?"

"He's looking for more ammo against Posner. I usually try to stay even between White and Posner, but I'm loading my hand on White's side this time. You're my ace in the hole."

"If either you or White want my help, I want to know more about what's going on between them."

Jake told me there was a long-standing animosity between Posner and White, but didn't go into any detail as to why. He said he didn't know, but I didn't believe him.

He'd been given some outside information that things were leaning more in White's direction, so he'd opted to lean that way a bit more. He just had to be able to cover his ass if this didn't turn out in his favor.

My opinion of Jake completely changed during that conversation. I hadn't lost my attraction to him, but I understood him a bit better. He was nothing like my partners at

White and Associates. He lived an entirely different life, constantly watching his back. He and I were more alike than I had ever thought we could be.

The bond I now felt with Jake didn't add to my trust of him, but detracted from it. His flaws were more evident. His only motivation was himself. I'd found myself in the same position more than once since leaving White and Associates. And if I wanted to be truthful with myself, I'd been doing the same since Colin and my dad cut me off. I looked past the Danny incident. The facts were all in front of me, but I didn't give them a second thought after my initial impression something was wrong. I should have figured it out, but I chose not to.

No, I trusted him even less, now that I knew we were more alike.

Jake gave me a tour later that evening and told me what my job would entail.

The crew ran in eight hour shifts, and I'd be standing guard on the wall every second shift from here on out. That meant I'd get up on the wall early in the afternoon and I'd be relieved around ten o'clock every night.

"I've gone entire stints where everything was quiet, but that doesn't mean we won't see any action," Jake said.

"What is it I'm supposed to find for White?"

He shook his head and smiled.

"I don't know. You'll have to pay attention."

I didn't believe he didn't know, but I knew I wouldn't get it out of him.

Chapter Twenty-One

THE NEXT AFTERNOON, I FOUND myself in a tower with a man I'd never met before. He introduced himself as John and we didn't speak again.

The tower air was stagnant. The bulletproof glass that separated us from the outside of the refinery stopped any air circulation. Thankfully, we had a vent near the ceiling that pushed out a little breeze. I was sure John and I would be dead from heat exhaustion if it weren't for that little vent.

I searched the yard for Joe and Eric, but they weren't anywhere to be seen. I did see Jake from time to time. He didn't have a wall position. Instead, he was roaming the grounds, making sure everything was in its place. When I asked him about it later, he confirmed that Joe had the morning shift and Eric was on the night shift.

The heat and humidity were almost unbearable as I stood at my position. The view of the surrounding forest and the river kept the job interesting. Birds flitted through the trees, and every once in a while a swirl in the muddy river made me wonder what was below the surface.

This continued for more than two months. Birds, heat, humidity, quiet. After my shift, I'd go to my room and stay there. Jake followed me for the first few days, but when he couldn't persuade me to join him in the commons room, he started leaving me alone in my room. Every morning I'd rise with the sun and take a run around the refinery.

I kept watch for something to report to White. At one point I'd tried to do a little side exploring in my time off. Most of the refinery was open to me, but there was one building that was heavily guarded. I wasn't allowed to get within fifty feet of it. The behavior was suspicious, but it didn't mean there was something worth reporting back to White. I suspected Jake had just told White there was something in the works in hopes of getting something in return. It worked out for Jake either way. If I failed to report anything, I was the one who failed, and, at least, he'd tried to give White the information he wanted.

I'd given up my search for anything illicit long before the day Jake told us all to be extra diligent. Apparently, the owner of the refinery was coming in sometime today.

I had six shifts left, then I was on my own. I still hadn't decided what I was going to do. My mind had strayed, every day, to thoughts of White. I wondered how he was coping without Will. I had an apartment I was welcome to use that allowed me easy access to White, as well as the rest of my partners. I still hadn't decided if I'd stay long-term at my apartment, but I had decided I would go back.

My nervousness at seeing Red was gone. I'd worked out exactly what I'd tell him if he tried to speak with me. I'd simply hear his opening statement, then tell him I had no interest in speaking to him ever again. I'd realized, after staying for a day at my apartment, I missed the men. Though I loved working with them, it was their company I missed the most. The attitude had changed. I was no longer a subordinate, I was a colleague. Okay, maybe not a colleague, but they'd treated me like a respected peer. I could handle that, as long as they didn't ask too much about my comings and goings.

Another decision I'd halfway made was my fate at Mesa. I would put them on the back burner for a time. Depending on how many jobs I could get on my own, I might never go back to working with them. However, I intended to keep Jake on my radar. Hopefully, I could do that without taking on jobs or promising sex.

Colin was a worrisome prospect. We hadn't spoken in months and that easy friendship we'd always had was harder and harder to access with long periods of time to distance us. Thinking of what I may have lost with Colin practically killed me. Our lives had taken different roads. The only thing I could do was get back in touch with him. Maybe I could work things out with him, too. It was time to put everything behind me. Hold onto nothing and start over. It was amazing what a person could think through in three months, if left to herself.

Through all my worrying and wondering about my partners, White, and Colin, I'd also worked through several scenarios of attack. Jake had told us to be extra diligent because the owner would be here, so I ran through everything again.

Figuring out a defense strategy was easier after I'd worked out how I would infiltrate.

If the attackers had long-range rifles, those of us on the wall would be easy targets. I scanned the tallest trees, even though that was probably the least likely scenario.

If I had the resources, I would never do a ground attack on this refinery. The refinery was protected by a thick swath of open area on all sides as well as the river on the south side. It would be safer to drop in from the sky.

The dock was another touchy place, though a rougher entry than a night drop. Divers could easily make landfall on our side of the river before detection. However, getting to the gates untouched might be nearly impossible. Still, an attacking force could easily infiltrate the ships waiting to transport the oil and launch an attack from the ship. If they had some serious firepower, they could, more than likely, take the refinery. Still, more dangerous than a night drop into the middle of the refinery, where things weren't well guarded. A couple well-placed snipers on top of the storage tanks could take out most of the opposition.

There were ways. The question was, did our attackers have the resources and training to pull it off?

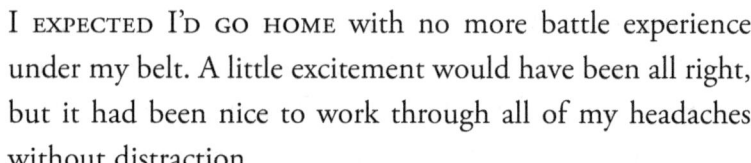

I EXPECTED I'D GO HOME with no more battle experience under my belt. A little excitement would have been all right, but it had been nice to work through all of my headaches without distraction.

The first thing I'd do when I got home was go down and visit with Gabriella. I wondered how her reception had turned out.

Movement inside the refinery caught my attention and made me drop all other thought.

A group came into view with Bud and another man leading the pack. It looked like Bud was explaining things to the other man.

He must be the owner.

But, how had he gotten into the refinery? No boats had docked all day. I hadn't heard a chopper land near the refinery. I was stumped.

As they drew closer, I realized I recognized the man up front with Bud. At first I only knew he looked familiar, but I couldn't remember from where. When I took a quick look at the group with my scope it came back to me. It was the cartel leader, Mateo Ruiz. The same man I'd taken pictures of in Jamaica, when White and I took a job as an excuse to get in some romance.

This must be what Jake had told me to keep an eye out for. Mesa was working for a drug dealer we'd previously done surveillance on. This *had* to be what Jake wanted me to report back to White.

Ruiz and the rest of the men made a quick sweep of the area near my post, then disappeared around a corner. I stewed on it for the rest of my shift, anxious to get back to my room and give White a call.

The rest of my shift dragged on and I couldn't concentrate on the surrounding jungle. Finally, it was over and I went straight to my room.

Jake was in his room with our adjoining doors opened.

"Were you going through my things?" I asked.

"No. Just wanted to know the second you got back to your room. We need to talk."

"About what?"

"Ruiz. His presence isn't the whole story. You might want to wait and report directly to White."

"Why?" I didn't try to hide my suspicion.

"I don't know. I just have a feeling." He smiled at me, so I knew he had more than just a feeling.

"Let's watch some T.V. for a while," he said.

"Okay."

I switched on my television and flopped onto my bed. Jake took three steps and jumped onto the bed next to me and grabbed up the remote.

While he flipped through the channels he asked, "Are you going to be staying at your apartment at White and Associates when you get home?"

"That's my current plan," I said.

"Good. I just want to know where I can find you when I get back."

"You aren't coming back with me?"

"No. I imagine I'm going to be here a couple extra days."

Nothing more was said because he'd found something on TV he was interested in. I couldn't get into the show and told him I wanted to go to bed. He didn't argue, but insisted we leave the adjoining doors open.

I wondered what he was planning, so I didn't argue with him, either. I shut off my television and watched him walk back to his room.

He switched on his own television, but turned the volume down low enough I could barely hear it. Still, I couldn't stay asleep. I dozed and then woke with a start several times.

The last time I did this I actually woke up to Jake standing over my bed.

I sat up stiffly and demanded he tell me what he was doing.

"I was coming in to wake you. Are you going to be upset if I make you leave most of your stuff behind?"

"What do you mean? Leave my stuff behind? What's going on?"

Jake didn't answer me, but he didn't need to. Less than three seconds after I asked my question I heard a huge explosion.

"You have your weapons, right?" Jake asked.

"Yes. I've been sleeping with them," I answered. "What the hell was that?"

"We are under attack." He smiled. "I need you to get Ruiz to safety. Joe will go with you. You'll need this, too."

Jake handed me the rifle that had been sitting near my door since the day I broke out of the cell.

Someone pounded on Jake's door.

"It's open," Jake called out.

Joe stormed in. "Jake?"

"In here, Joe," Jake said as Joe walked further into the room.

"We've got to evacuate Ruiz," Joe said. He also held a rifle.

"Yep. You and Alex will get him the hell out of here. I have to stay here and keep control of the refinery."

"Okay. Let's go, Alex," Joe said.

The two men shook hands briskly.

"We'll see you back at home in a few days. Watch your ass, buddy," Joe said.

"Get going."

I followed Joe out the door and down the hall. He pounded on another door and announced himself. Ruiz answered it immediately.

"We have to get you out of here, Mr. Ruiz," Joe said.

Ruiz only nodded and stepped out of his room.

"We don't have time to wait for your regular detail. I'll take the lead, you stay between me and Ms. Grey. Understood?" Joe asked him.

"Let's go," Ruiz said.

The three of us took the one flight of stairs to the first floor and made our way outside.

I heard scattered gunfire as Joe led us deeper into the refinery. He led us directly to the building I'd been denied access to earlier in my stay.

The guards hadn't budged from their posts and didn't offer any objections when we raced past them into the building.

Once inside, I couldn't understand why I'd been denied access. It was nothing more than a storage building, with not a whole lot stored in it.

Joe continued further into the building and down some stairs I hadn't seen. We ended up going down five flights before ever reaching a door. Another pair of guards stood at the foot of the stairs, guns at the ready. When they saw Joe, they relaxed and allowed us passage.

We hurried into a huge, underground setup. I immediately realized this was where they *refined* the drugs. The place was huge and doused in bright white lights. There were at least a hundred workers doing various things. I wouldn't have had any idea of what was going on if I hadn't seen some of them packing a white powder into bags and then stacking them onto pallets. That, and knowing Ruiz's true occupation, made the deduction an easy one. This was a drug factory.

After we'd walked into the factory a few hundred feet, Joe took a sharp right turn and led us toward another guarded door.

We were allowed entry without hesitation once again. The scene on the other side of the door was a shock to me. We were in an underground garage filled with different kinds of ATVs.

Joe ushered Ruiz into a side-by-side and instructed me to get into the back. As soon as I was in, he took off down a tunnel that could have held a full sized SUV.

We drove at top speed for at least half an hour. None of us said anything until Joe slowed down and spoke into his radio.

"It's Joe. We had some trouble at the refinery. Open the gate. We're evacuating Ruiz."

Within seconds of his call, I saw a light up ahead. A garage door of sorts was lifting up. It was fully open by the time we reached it and we drove up a steep ramp into an airplane hangar.

The hangar held two small planes and several armed men. Two of them escorted us onto one of the planes as the hangar doors opened up. As we strapped into our seats, the airplane taxied out onto the runway and was in the air before I could ask where we were going.

Joe had been on his phone since we entered the plane.

"What the hell happened back there?" Ruiz demanded of Joe after we'd been in the air for a few minutes.

Joe held up his finger at Ruiz and took a few seconds to end his phone call.

I'd been staring out one of the windows at the stars, wondering how our guys were faring in the gun battle.

"I'm not sure," Joe said.

"I can't afford to lose that refinery," Ruiz said.

"I was just talking with Jake and our men already have the situation under control." Joe said. "He'll have a full report for Posner when he wraps things up. I'm sure Mark will fill you in."

Ruiz's temper had already calmed and he thanked Joe for acting so fast to get him out of there. He clapped a hand on Joe's shoulder and gave me a nod of thanks before he moved toward the back of the plane.

After a couple minutes, I asked Joe where we were going.

"We'll land soon at Ruiz's private airstrip. He'll disembark and then we'll head home."

"Do you know what happened back there? Is everyone okay?"

"Jake said it was the barge. Someone placed charges on the barge and walked away from it. There was no further attack."

He shrugged.

I was too tired to ask any more questions. After we dropped Ruiz off at his private airstrip, Joe went to the back of the plane to get some sleep, and I napped in my seat.

Chapter Twenty-Two

J OE OFFERED ME A RIDE after we landed. When we got on
the road he asked where he should drop me off.

"White and Associates."

"You going back to them?"

He took his eyes off the road to stare wide-eyed at me for
a few seconds.

"No." I shook my head. "I have an apartment there. It's
cleaner than hotel rooms and it's a nice central location."

"Ah. Makes sense. Might not be the best choice, though.
I don't think you should go back there right now."

"Why not?"

"Posner. If he finds out you're staying there, he'll probably cut you off. Or worse," he said.

"I'm taking a break from Mesa. I don't like doing jobs I know so little about."

"What're you going to do?" he asked.

"Not sure." I shrugged.

I wondered if Joe knew more details about what happened at the refinery. How much did he know about Mesa? How much did he know about Jake? Was I the only one without a clue?

"Joe?" I asked. "What do you know about the job we did with Danny?"

"Ah. Pretty much everything. I was there," he said.

"Were you in on the plan for me to shoot Danny?"

"Yep." His tone was blasé.

I shook my head.

"What?" he asked with innocence in his voice. "We all needed to know if you'd step up. We couldn't have taken you with us to Sudan if we didn't know."

"Yeah. I suppose my word isn't good enough."

"Come on, Alex. You'd told Posner you wouldn't shoot anyone. He had to know if you would in a pinch. You did great."

"Except I shot an unarmed man," I said.

"Danny was a punk and if you hadn't done it, someone else would have. Me, in fact."

"Did you know we were doing the hit for Ruiz?" I was prodding. I had no idea if Ruiz had paid for the hit, but I knew he would be in a position to ask for the action.

"Of course. Why so many questions, Alex?" He narrowed his eyes at me.

"Just curious about how much everyone knew. I must have been the only one in the dark on all our jobs. Makes me wonder what the catch was with each of them."

"That was the only one that had any hidden agenda. Promise."

"What about the refinery? I had no idea it wasn't just an oil refinery. And, that explosion seemed more than a little convenient."

"Well, the refinery is what it is. We don't tell anyone what goes on underground. And, the explosion—" He shrugged and smiled. "If Jake has an opportunity to gain control over Mesa, I'll be his second in command."

"You're saying Jake planted those explosives?"

"Nope. Not saying that—out loud."

"This is why I'm going to try and do things on my own for a while. I can't stand all this bullshit. I say, pick a side and defend it," I said.

"What do you mean? I've picked a side."

"Really?" I was unconvinced.

"Yep. I'm on Jake's side. You should know, he's taking a huge risk so you can get this information to White. That's why I don't think you staying there is such a good idea. If Posner finds out you're there, he's going to take it out on Jake first."

"I'm not going to be working with them, I'm just going to live in *my* apartment."

"Try explaining that to Posner. You were Jake's pet project. He backed you. If you go back to that apartment, Posner is going to assume you were nothing but a spy and Jake was either duped or in on it. Either way, it's not good for Jake."

"Why didn't Jake tell me this? He knew I planned on going back to my apartment."

"Maybe he really was duped?"

This statement made me scowl. I'd never once been unclear of my feelings. Mesa was a place for me to kill time. I'd even made that clear to Posner.

Damn it. I had no doubts Posner would take things to the extreme if he thought someone was selling information about his company. But, it wasn't *my* plan to put me in a position to get information for White. Technically, I wasn't the spy. Jake was.

These men only did things for their own benefit. Yet, Mark Posner had some very nasty habits, and maybe this was the best way these men could take a stand. I might not approve of hiding in the shadows, but—hiding in the shadows was what I did best. Who did I think I was kidding? If anyone ever had a questionable job, it was me. Who was I to judge?

"So, you think I should go back to hotel rooms?"

"No. I think you need to go back to Mesa. At least for a while."

My stomach dropped. If I cared what happened to him and Jake, I should, at least, consider going back to Mesa for a time. Or, I could opt to keep the refinery information to myself.

"I can take you to White and Associates and then back to Mesa with me," Joe said.

"I didn't ask for this. All I wanted was a job outside of White and Associates. One that did the right thing, without breaking the law. I'm *never* going to get what I want."

"So, is that a yes?"

"Let me talk to White, first. But, probably."

Joe was quiet for the remainder of the drive, giving me a chance to work through it in my mind. Going back to Mesa was my only choice, unless I could talk Jake into skipping the country with me. That was something I'd never ask of him. I didn't want to give him the wrong idea, but I felt compelled to protect him. Even if he did get himself into this position.

Joe parked on the street outside White and Associates.

"I'll come in with you? Help you get what you need from your apartment?"

I closed my eyes and took a deep breath.

"Okay. But, I might only stay until Jake gets back from the refinery."

"You're doing the right thing, Alex."

PHIL WAS ON DUTY. He picked up his phone as soon as he saw Joe and me walk in.

"Ms. Grey," he greeted me with a somber voice.

"Everything okay, Phil?"

He held up his hand and spoke into the phone. "She's here."

He hung up the phone before he redirected his attention back to me.

"Your partners will be waiting for you in the office. I'm sorry."

"Sorry for what?"

What the hell have I done now?

"Nothing, ma'am."

He was obviously shaken and knew something I didn't. I opted not to hound him and just go up and find out what was going on.

My hands started to shake and I gave Joe a sidelong glance as we waited for the elevator.

"I don't know what's going on, Joe. But you might want to go back to the car."

"I'm sure it's fine," he said.

By the time the elevator opened up to the seventh floor, my senses were heightened. My breathing was more shallow and my heart raced.

"Hi, Gabriella," I said when we walked into the office.

"Hi, hon. They're waiting for you."

The look of sorrow on her face only served to agitate me further. I wanted to grill her about what was going on, but I saw all of my partners standing in White's office.

Joe and I walked past Gabriella and Red's voice came to my ears.

"Ms. Grey," he greeted me.

I unintentionally glared and didn't answer him. He stood behind White's desk with the rest of the men standing near him.

"Where's White? I'm supposed to deliver some information to him."

I was visibly shaking now.

"He's not here," Red said.

"I'm not asking you, Red," I spit out.

I looked at Black. "Where's White?"

Black shook his head and looked at the ground.

I looked around the room and they all wore looks of pure agony. "Brown? Where is White?" I was beginning to panic.

Red's voice grated in my ears.

"He's gone, Alex."

"Fuck off, Red! Black. Where is he?" I pleaded.

"Alex," Brown came to my side. "For some reason, he thought Will was still alive. He left to find him without telling any of us. The Admiral called a couple months ago and confirmed that he'd been killed."

"What do you mean? Where is he?"

Joe put his hand on my shoulder.

"Don't—" I turned to face Joe and he backed away a couple steps.

"He's not gone. He's out there somewhere. Why aren't you all out there helping him look for Will?"

"Alex," Black's voice commanded all of my attention.

I looked at him and he held my gaze. He didn't need to say a word. His eyes said it all. White wasn't missing. My eyes filled with tears as I looked into Black's face. This could not be happening. This was not real.

The fear I'd felt when I watched Ruben shoot White rushed over me, followed by an even deeper fear I didn't know was possible. How could I live without him? How? This was *not* real.

My eye contact with Black was the only thing holding me upright. His face was the only thing I could see. Nothing mattered any more. What was the point?

I tried to tell Black to go to hell. I tried to shake my head, as if saying no would make it go away. But I couldn't move. I couldn't breathe. The only thing I could feel were the tears streaming down my cheeks and the absolute despair that filled me.

My vision of Black's face started to falter and move further away. The ringing in my ears became deafening, and I felt my knees buckle. The normal jarring feeling that comes when your knees give out was absent and so was the pain when my knees hit the floor. Everything was black now. I expected to feel the floor on my face, but it never came.

Instead, I heard tinny voices as my senses came back little by little.

I found myself hunched over my knees on the floor and the men were arguing about something.

I didn't mean to, but I let out a slight sound as the headache hit me.

Blue was by my side and helped me sit up. The room had become quiet again.

"Can you stand?" he asked.

I shook my head no, but it wasn't in response to his question. I still couldn't fully process what was going on. There was no way this was really happening. I got to my feet with a little help from Blue on my left and another pair of hands on my right.

"We'll take you to your apartment," Blue said.

"No," Joe interrupted. "She's coming with me."

I now knew it was Joe who'd been the other pair of hands helping me stand, because I felt as if I were in the middle of a tug-of-war.

Black saved me and led me to the couch. Everyone's voices still held a bit of a metallic ring to them, but my ears were starting to clear up. I sat on the couch with my head in my hands until Red's voice cropped up directly in front of me.

"Alex? Are you going to be okay?" he asked.

My anger with Red multiplied a million times. I let my hands drop and I looked him directly in the face. That smug, self-satisfied face he dared put within my reach.

"Red," I said through sobs. "You're asking me if I'm going to be okay when it's because of you I didn't get to be with White? YOU?" I struck out and had him on the ground in seconds. I screamed at him as I pummeled him. "Months!" I yelled. "I lost MONTHS. And now I'll never be able to get them back. NEVER!" I intended to kill him with my bare hands. I sat on his chest and stopped punching him and slipped his shoulders under my knees and proceeded to strangle him. He fought, but I had him. My partners would have two people to mourn.

"I *will* kill you," I growled as his face started to turn blue.

My triumph didn't last long before Black lifted me off Red. If it had been anyone else lifting me off him, I would have fought them. I crumpled in his arms and he held me tightly.

Red coughed on the floor for a couple of seconds before he took his place behind White's desk again.

When my sobs settled down and I stood motionless in Blacks arms, he quietly asked if I wanted to go to my apartment or go with Joe.

"Joe," I whispered.

Black's grip didn't loosen as he led me out of the office and onto the elevator with Joe in tow.

Chapter Twenty-Three

"I REALLY THOUGHT THEY WERE GOING to let you kill him," Joe said after he'd led me to my room at Mesa.

I didn't answer him. I'd already forgotten my attack on Red. My mind was swimming in thoughts of White.

"What the hell did he do to make them just stand there while you beat the shit out of him and almost kill him?"

"Doesn't matter. He's dead now, anyway. Please, just leave me alone," I said.

"I'll come and get you when it's time to brief Posner. I'm sure he's going to want to get our version before Jake shows up," Joe said.

"Fine."

"You going to hold it together, Alex?"

"I'm fine." I took in a shaky breath.

"Keep in mind, Posner doesn't know where we stopped first and if he knows you still have such deep ties, it could be problematic."

Joe left me alone in my room with a promise to return soon.

I went to bed, hoping to sleep the time away. I fought my emotions, but managed to contain the tears even though I couldn't fall asleep.

"JOE, ALEX," POSNER GREETED US when we walked into his office.

"Please, take your seats."

We did as we were told and he asked us to fill him in on what happened.

Our stories were similar. We were both off shift and woke up to an explosion. At which time, we hurried to usher Ruiz to safety.

"Why you two and not anyone else?" Posner asked me.

"I'm not sure. I do know we were the first to reach his room and Jake opted to stay behind to fight for the refinery. It happened pretty fast."

"Okay. Thank you both for acting so quickly." He turned his attention to Joe. "As soon as Jake arrives, I want him here."

I followed Joe's lead and rose from my seat.

"Understood," Joe said.

Back in my room, Joe said, "Glad to see you can put things behind you."

I just nodded and asked him to leave. He didn't argue.

Once I was alone I curled up on my bed and cried myself to sleep.

JAKE'S FACE CAME INTO VIEW as he shook me.

"Alex," he said. "You need to get up. Joe says you've been in bed since you got here. You *need* to get up."

My mouth was dry and I could barely speak. "Why? What's going on?" I barely had the strength to sit up.

"You've been in bed for five days."

White.

I leaned over the edge of the bed and dry heaved for a couple minutes while Jake rubbed my back. When my body gave up on trying to purge the nothingness that inhabited my stomach, Jake pulled me close to him and I cried.

"It's okay. It'll be okay," he said.

I WOKE UP IN JAKE'S arms. He was curled up next to me, holding me tight. I tried to get out from under his grasp without waking him, but didn't manage it.

"Alex? What's wrong?"

"I need to use the bathroom,"

"Oh, good."

He let go and I sat up. It was hard work and I was shaking.

"After you're done in there, I'll take you out for something to eat. I'm sure you could use some fresh air as much as you need food. You've actually lost weight since I saw you last."

I TOOK A LONG, HOT shower. My mind wouldn't stop replaying every single moment I'd spent with White until I wondered how he died. What'd happened? Why did he think Will was still alive? Did he have proof or was it his grief pushing him?

If he had proof, it couldn't have been strong enough for any of the colors to agree with him. Why did he do this? I had to know what happened.

When I exited the bathroom in my towel, Jake was sitting on the edge of my bed. I considered worrying about what he might see, but decided I didn't care.

"I need to find out what happened," I said.

Jake didn't pay my towel any attention and spoke to me as if I was fully dressed.

"I talked briefly with Black. He said White was acting strangely. He even got all his affairs in order."

"You think he did this on purpose?"

Just the thought pissed me off. White would never do that.

"No, but he did think he might never come back. Why don't you give me a second and I'll see if one of your partners can meet us for dinner."

"It better not be Red."

"Yeah, I know. Joe told me how you just about killed him and no one tried all that hard to stop you."

Jake stepped out of my bedroom and shut the door. I assumed he did that so I could get dressed in private.

I dropped my towel and caught my reflection in the dresser mirror. I had lost weight. I'd have a bit of work to do if I wanted to get back some of my muscle.

I shrugged on some clothes and stepped out of the room. Jake was just concluding a phone call.

"Green said he'll meet us. You ready?"

As we drove to meet Green, I asked him how things turned out at the refinery and what he told Posner.

"I just told him the truth. Someone must have placed that charge on the barge as a diversion. Not sure why they didn't attempt to follow through. Maybe the charge went off before they were ready. At least we got Ruiz out of there."

"I haven't given anyone the information you wanted me to give White."

"Not a big deal. I need to create a relationship with another one of your partners now, anyway."

I swallowed my sorrow.

"I'm sorry, Alex. I know this is hard for you. It's hard for me, too. I really respected White."

"It's okay, Jake."

GREEN WAS ALREADY AT THE table. He rose to greet us.

"Jake. Alex."

I nodded my hello and Jake reached out to shake his hand. Green responded with a brief handshake.

"You've gotten thin," he said as soon as we sat.

I shrugged it off. "I need to know what happened."

"I know. I'm not really sure. He just up and disappeared. None of us even knew where he was until Red went into his apartment and found a note. It just said he went to get Will. We spent a month looking for him. Then the Admiral called and said he had it on good authority that White was killed trying to break into a well-protected compound."

"What compound?" I asked.

"The Admiral wouldn't say, and we tried to get him to talk. Red's still trying to get the details."

"Excuse me, please," I said as I left the table.

"Let me know what he says," Green called after me.

I walked to the ladies restroom and checked the stalls. I was alone.

I called my dad.

"Hello?"

"Hi, dad," I said.

"Alex."

I could picture his haughty expression.

"It's been a while. How have you been? I hear you've been working with the undesirables over at Mesa."

"I want to know what happened to White."

"I'm sorry, honey."

His tone completely changed and he was very sympathetic.

"What happened?"

"I've already told your boy, Red, everything I know."

"Red is *not* my boy, and I don't believe you. What compound was White trying to break into and why did he have reason to believe Will might still be alive?"

"You ready to give up Red, then?"

"There's nothing to give up. But, just so you know, if I have any further problems with Red, he'll not be causing anyone else any problems. Now, I want to know what happened to White."

"Sweetie—"

"Don't sweetie me. Just tell me what compound and why."

"I don't know. I received a communication from one of our contacts in Brazil. He told me White was caught trying to break into a highly guarded government facility. He assumed White had gone rogue and brought the break-in to my attention before it could become an international incident."

"What compound?"

"He refused to tell me."

"Why would White think his little brother was still alive?" I asked.

"It might have something to do with the fact that we never did recover his body. People do strange things when they are grieving. Speaking of, why don't you come home for a while?"

"No. I'm not coming home, but I will give you the information that I was meant to bring back to White. I recently did a stint as a security guard at an oil refinery down in South

America as part of a Mesa team. Turns out the oil refinery is also a drug refinery and is owned by Ruiz. I thought this might be information you could use since you had us do some surveillance on Ruiz several months back. This ties Posner and Ruiz together."

"I already knew they worked together. You snapped me some nice pictures of Mesa security down in Jamaica. Where is this refinery?"

"Somewhere in South America. My sources didn't tell me exactly where it was, sorry."

"You just said you were on the team," he said.

"Did I? Wanna trade information?"

"What? You're bargaining with me? Alex—" His volume had escalated before he took a breath. "I'll let you know when I'm ready to trade," he said in a more controlled tone.

He hung up on me.

I stormed out of the restroom and back to the table. By the time I reached Green and Jake, I'd expended the little surge of energy I'd gotten from my anger. I was shaking when I sat down.

"You need to get some food," Jake said.

"What did he say, Alex?" Green asked.

"Who?" Jake interrupted.

"The Admiral," I answered him.

"You have a direct line to the Admiral?" Jake was incredulous.

I rolled my eyes and sighed.

"He wouldn't tell me anything either, but I have a little tidbit of info I can hold over his head. Not sure if it's good enough information to get him to talk, though. Only time will tell. Let the guys know I'll keep on him," I told Green.

"Good. If there's anything I can do to help you, let me know," Green said.

He stood from the table and left me alone with Jake.

"You know the Admiral? I mean, I knew you'd worked for him, but so do a lot of other people. They don't get a direct line to him."

"It's no big deal, Jake. He's an ass, anyway."

"I knew that, and I've never had a conversation with him. But, he's a connected ass. You need to stay on good terms with him. He can make or break you. He's more ruthless than Posner."

"The Admiral knows more than he's telling me. I'll find out what it is and then, whoever is responsible for this, is dead."

I didn't say this for Jake's benefit. It was a simple fact. When I found out who'd killed White, no matter what the reason, they'd cease to exist.

THE END

About the Author

J.C. PHELPS IS A WIFE and mother of three who writes from the beautiful Black Hills of South Dakota.

Somehow, in the middle of the chaos of caring for her daughters, a growing collection of chickens, ducks, and geese, and tending a large garden, she finds the time to write.

The Alexis Stanton Chronicles have been the most enjoyable works she's written. *Color Me Grey*, the first book in the series, introduces the characters she has come to love.

Discover other titles by J.C. Phelps at your
favorite online bookseller!

The Alexis Stanton Chronicles

Color Me Grey
Shades of Grey
Reflections of Grey
Traces of Grey

Connect with the author online

Facebook

J.C. Phelps

Email

authorjcphelps@yahoo.com

Blog

http://jcphelps.blogspot.com

Website

www.msgrey.com

www.ingramcontent.com/pod-product-compliance
Lightning Source LLC
Chambersburg PA
CBHW072210170626
46813CB00003B/876